T0157334

MICKEY SWAGER

MICKEY SWAGER

REMI ARTS

Archway Publishing books may be ordered through booksellers or by contacting:

Archway Publishing
1663 Liberty Drive
Bloomington, IN 47403
www.archwaypublishing.com
1 (888) 242-5904

ISBN: 978-1-4808-7984-3 (sc)
ISBN: 978-1-4808-7985-0 (e)

Library of Congress Control Number: 2019908963

Print information available on the last page.

Archway Publishing rev. date: 07/09/2019

ACKNOWLEDGMENT

Without extraordinary understanding,
encouragement, and editing,
my story could never
have come this far.

Thank you, Beverly,
my ingenium secreto.

1

The San

Scratching a hole in the ice on the window, I watched the cold winter landscape pass by. Houses, bridges, and roads would soon disappear, and I'd be in the mountains north of Montreal, well known for their colorful fall display as well as their ski slopes in the winter. I'd been there in the spring when crisp, clear water bounced wildly along the rocks in the creeks and streams. In summer, the water receded to a mere trickle, but everything was lush, green and alive; people were happy to escape the city and spend time in the Laurentian mountains.

It was November 1957. The excitement among the skiers headed for the slopes was high, in direct contrast to my own. My freedom was about to be taken away. I was on my way to a sanatorium. Pleading with my parents to find a way of keeping me home hadn't changed anything. I felt that I was being banished.

The rocking of the train caused my father to close his eyes and escape the reality of the situation, for he was a gentle person but all too willing to let my mother make the decisions of the family.

His head bobbed back and forth while my mother, a devout Catholic, sat with her head bowed as the beads of her rosary slipped slowly through her fingers. Her lips moved soundlessly. She was probably thinking of her sister who had died of TB many years before. I remember my aunt's tale of woe enough times not to want to suffer the same fate. I tried to kill myself in a failed attempt after being diagnosed with TB. The botched episode to crash my car was in hindsight probably a last minute change of heart. I drove the rest of the way home contemplating on how to deliver the devastating news to my parents.

The window had frosted over again. The train stopped, and some of the skiers excitedly got off. I knew that when my time came to disembark, my feelings would be anything but elation. Although I didn't like my home, I knew nothing else so leaving it scared the crap out of me. Looking at my mother sitting across from me, I realized that I didn't love her. I knew that she loved my father very much but I didn't feel that she loved me, or any of my siblings for that matter. I remembered the day while still at home waiting for a bed in the sanatorium when much to her surprise I had asked her if she loved me. I should have known her answer before asking it because she never mentioned love or showed any affection to her children. None in our household ever hugged. Still, I hoped that this time it would be different.

"Of course, I love you. You're one of my children."

"That wasn't what I meant. Do love me because I am your son or because I am who I am?"

"Don't be so difficult, Mickey, I said that I love my children and that should be enough," she answered impatiently. It was clear that these types of questions made her feel uncomfortable. I recalled another incident when I had asked some questions about girls and sex. She was visibly embarrassed and answered curtly:

"There isn't any reason for you to know about these things, you'll find out when you're older."

Interesting enough she was the trailblazer of the family, considered to be an intellectual. People regularly came to her for advice. After all, she had written and published two children's books, and she wrote a regular short-story column for children. But she had little time for her own children and left them ignorant.

"*SAINEGAT!*" yelled the conductor. This was the end of the line for me. Looking through the open door, I saw the sign on the old wooden train station. It read: "Ste Agathe des Monts."

Would I be like my Aunt Celia, wheezing, and walking tilted to one side, if so, it would have been better if I'd died in the car crash?

We stood on the wooden platform, and the train rumbled on. A taxi stood waiting to take us to the *San,* as the sanatorium was called by everyone.

It was an ugly red brick building, three stories high with a flat roof. The two top floors had black-screened balconies that ran the full length of the building. The dark-green paint on the front doors and on the small window frames of the ground floor was peeling and blistered. It looked more like a jail than a hospital. A snow plow was clearing the driveway and the parking lot. The whole atmosphere was cold and impersonal, and I didn't have any illusions about the inside to be any more inviting.

The smell of disinfectant met us when we entered the building. The gray terrazzo floors, beige walls with green trim, was even more depressing. There wasn't a picture anywhere to be seen. Plants or flowers would have made a difference, but they too were missing from the décor. Nothing had been done to make it homier. It was a typical institution and going to be my home for at least a year, although the doctor at the clinic in the city had forewarned me that it could be much longer.

Mom spoke to the receptionist through a little hole in the glass. She was pretty but didn't smile. My mom and dad were allowed to go with me. We passed a man in a white shirt and pants, mopping the floor. He stopped for a moment to let us pass. He stood wheezing, tilted to one side. The elevator took us to the third floor where we waited at the nurses' station. After a minute or so, an older nurse came out from one of the rooms and introduced herself as Nurse Tang, head nurse. Her smile was nothing more than a twitch. She took the bag that my father was carrying and commented on how little I had brought, considering the length of time I would be there. She said that it was better to say our goodbyes right away so she could get me to bed as soon as possible. It was an awkward moment. I wasn't sure what to say to my parents; there really wasn't anything to say, after all, I had put the welfare of the family in jeopardy. Dad extended his hand and shook mine vigorously. Mom pecked my cheek, and they left quickly.

It was my first time away from home and reality struck when the elevator door closed behind them. The motto "men don't cry" flashed through my mind, and I bit my lower lip.

I followed Nurse Tang down the hall. Patients in dressing gowns and pajamas stood in doorways and leaned against the walls. Most were old. There were also a few younger faces, but I didn't see anyone my own age. She took me to the end of the hall to a room with three older patients and said that she would see to it that I was placed with boys closer to my age. I really didn't care. The room was as cold and impersonal as the rest of the place. A small light fixture, mounted on the wall over the bed, looked like an upside-down soup ladle. It was painted the same beige color as the wall. The beds were old, and half the light green paint was rubbed off from numerous sterilizations. After changing into my pajamas and putting my things in the locker, I climbed into bed. The patient in the next bed coughed and spat in a little metal box with a cardboard lining inside it. He closed the lid and put the box back on his nightstand. It made me feel like puking. The same spit boxes were on the other nightstands, including mine. The room had no other furniture except for an uncomfortable metal chair that came with each bed. There were no cushions on the chairs because it was too hard to sterilize them. Skinny patients used their blankets for a bit of comfort. There were no tables, which was why a wooden tray with folding legs was our dining table, craftwork table or vanity for those who couldn't leave their beds. A small speaker plugged into the wall provided entertainment, limited as it was. A pull on a little chain attached to the wall switch brought up one of four radio stations. The volume wasn't adjustable; it could only be heard by holding it against your ear or putting it under the pillow.

Nurse Tang came back a few minutes later. Her face was expressionless. Her attempt to smile had obviously been for the benefit of my parents. I would soon learn that she had a reputation for scaring the new patients. She stood beside my bed to give me the rules and regulations, and a small jar.

"Here," she said, "use this for your sputum instead of your box."

"I don't need it, ma'am, I don't have to cough."

"Try anyway if not you'll have to go down to the lab tomorrow before breakfast ... the tube down your nose will get the same results. We'll need to test every week to see when your condition turns negative. You'll have to keep your distance from visitors until then."

She left me with the jar and the fear of the tube.

Un-assessed, considered contagious and seriously ill I was to stay in bed at all times. The only exception was the bathroom. I thought that it was a bit excessive because I didn't feel ill, I just felt very tired and sweaty.

Her warning about keeping a distance didn't make much sense when I saw how the other patients behaved. Neither nurses, orderlies, nor the girls who served our puky meals showed any concern about being infected.

At 5 feet 11 inches tall and weighing 115 pounds, I was skinny. At midday, my body temperature was 100.6. I didn't find out about the cavities in my lungs until I had been there a week; that news was another unexpected blow. The only activity I was allowed was reading. The librarian came by one day, her wagon was loaded with books, but when I thought about the bugs of coughing and spitting patients collected over time on the yellowing pages of all those books, I felt like barfing.

Huge quantities of pills were part of the cure. I was given 21 PAS (para-aminosalicylic acid) and INH (isoniazid) combined, per day. Patients who didn't respond to that were injected with streptomycin, an antibiotic. Nurse Tang said that my case was severe enough for the *strep* injections, but the doctor decided that my young age and otherwise healthy condition warranted trying the PAS-INH first.

Gaining weight was important, and patients were urged to eat as much as they could. The food, however, wasn't palatable enough and discouraged most from asking for seconds. Another part of the cure was being in bed outside on the balcony for five hours each day. The fact that it was November didn't matter. Without question or mercy, the beds were rolled outside, patients and all, no matter how cold it was.

My roommates were friendly, and my youth and ignorance seemed to give them a welcome change in a stagnant, boring environment. I was admitted on a Wednesday and the day for bathing was Friday. They started snickering, dropping hints and told me that I would be wheeled, bed and all, to the bathroom and given a bed-bath.

"Nursie is gonna wash you all over, even your balls."

I was panic-stricken, but there was no way out. I had to keep my cool or life would be impossible.

It was Friday morning, and my bed was rolled down the hall. My roommates gave me a special send-off, "keep it up, your spirit as well as your dick."

Nurse Tang stood in the doorway of the bathroom. Her smile sent chills down my spine. There was nothing worse than displaying ones' private parts. I was told that Nurse Tang took an extra long time washing *IT*. Oh God … what would I do if I were to get a hard-on while she was washing *IT*. No one other than myself had ever touched it before, even if you played with it, you had to confess your sin to the priest.

I squeezed *IT* hard enough under the blanket, along the hallway, to make my eyes water, hoping to save my dignity.

She was armed with a washcloth and paused for a moment … drawing out my agony. She pulled the sheet halfway down and started to wash. I was too embarrassed to look at her and tried to appear unbothered. She worked without saying a word until she washed My legs and saw my colorful knee. The usually pale skin had taken on the colors of a rainbow from bashing it against the steering column in my attempted suicide. She looked shocked.

"My God! What in the world happened to your knee, Mickey?"

"I … I slipped when I got into my car, and I banged my knee."

"I'll speak to the doctor; we'll have to take some X-rays."

"No, please, Miss Tang, I have been walking on it for a few days, and nothing is broken, it's just bruised."

She hesitated for a moment and had a better look.

"Okay, Mickey, but I want to keep an eye on it, okay?"

"It's too late for that, Miss Tang even a raw steak wouldn't do any good."

"Smart-ass, you know darn well what I mean."

She kept washing me and suddenly burst out laughing.

"Imagine being brought back to the ward with my eye on your knee."

I didn't think that it was that funny, but she must have because she kept laughing until she returned again from the sink. She stood and looked down at me and said with a straight face, "Now, my boy, the time has come."

I closed my eyes and felt my face go scarlet. Feeling helpless I prayed silently, "Oh God! Please, don't let me get a hard-on."

She suddenly slapped the wet cloth on my bare chest.

"You get to do the rest," she laughed out loud as she walked away.

"Scared the crap out of that boy', she announced passing the onlookers gathered in the hall.

I made up my mind to eventually get even with the old bat, considering my lengthy incarceration; I had enough time to plot.

I didn't usually fall asleep until early morning which made the nights long and lonely. Generally, I would lie there and stare into the dark, punctuated with snoring and coughing. I'd wait for the night nurse to do her rounds. Although her shoes made no sound, I could hear the rustling of her starched uniform. I couldn't see her face in the dark as she checked each bed, especially not when she directed the beam of her flashlight on me, and she stood still for a moment. The light blinded me, and I closed my eyes. The very faint smell of her perfume would linger for a while after she'd gone. One night she came and stood as before at the foot of my bed, but she turned her flashlight off. The moon was bright enough for me to see how pretty she was. I didn't think that she was really looking at me; I felt that she was only checking to see if I was still awake.

I fantasized about her after she was gone. That was about all I could do.

It was the night of December 9. This time she came back and stood for a moment. She was really looking at me. I wanted to speak to her, but I was too shy. Unbelievably, she came closer, looked down at me and ran her fingers through my hair. Then she bent over and whispered, "Sleep, Mickey, it will make the night shorter and less lonely."

She kissed my forehead, and I felt warm and special. How did she know that I was lonely?

The next evening she was back. My heart started beating even faster than before. I was awed by her actually taking notice of me. She was close enough for me to read her name tag and I whispered reading it, "Miss Lane."

She didn't want me to talk and put her finger to my lips, bent over and whispered in my ear. My heart was in my throat when her hair touched my face. My groin felt funny even though it was still sore from my self-mutilation.

"Call me Maggie, please and don't tell anyone about this or I will lose my job. Here read this and then destroy it."

She gave me a folded piece of paper and kissed my cheek. I felt strange. Was this a dream? If it were, I wanted it to go on forever, but she left. No girl had ever kissed me. When she was gone, I got out of bed and read the note under the tiny nightlight in the wall next to my bed.

Mickey, I can't help it. I have a crush on you. I can't explain it, but I can't help feeling this way. I have watched you night after night since the day you were admitted. I am probably making a fool of myself, but I have to take that chance.

Love, Maggie

I held onto the piece of paper like a treasure but realizing it wasn't safe I went to the bathroom and flushed it. I waited for her to come back on her second round and sat straight up in bed when she did. She checked on the others and saw that they were all sound asleep. I motioned for her to come. She leaned very close and put her arms around me. I held her and felt her breasts against me. It was a good feeling, and I wanted more, but she left. Walking away, she pulled something from her pocket and wiped her eyes. No one had ever hugged me. I thought that her hug and her breasts touching me was sex and I had probably sinned, but I didn't care. I wanted to feel more and explore these new feelings. At 20, I was still so very innocent. I grew up in the country and didn't even know how babies came to the world, other than when my mother was expecting, and the doctor came to our house and said that he had brought the baby in his bag.

I didn't see her for the next few nights because it was her time off. The next time she came in, I was lying propped on one elbow looking out the balcony doors. My heart started pounding as soon as she entered the room. Was I was falling in love? You bet! If I were growing up, it wasn't under the most favorable circumstances. Perhaps if I'd been adequately informed about these things, I would have understood that my feelings were normal. I would have known that wanting to touch her and hold her wasn't a sin.

I sat up against the pillows and stared at her. She leaned over and kissed my lips. I would have liked her to stay but each time she came was taking a risk. The rustle of her uniform was music to my ears, but it could awaken the others. I fell asleep as the light of a new day rose from behind the snowy mountains.

The days crept by. The temperature stayed below zero. My body was cold while out on that balcony, but my thoughts about Maggie were warm and gave me hope and strength.

It was getting close to Christmas, and my roommates were leaving for two weeks. Being too ill, I had to stay. Perhaps someone would come to visit and bring news from home. I'd heard about patients running away. It happened more often around Christmas. I was warned not to try it because the police would have me back in a jiffy. Besides, where would I go? I understood how scared my parents were. I could have infected someone else at home.

I lay down and listened to the speaker under my pillow. Bing Crosby was crooning, "I'll be home for Christmas." It made me homesick, and I tried my best not to get overly emotional. I kept reminding myself that crying was for girls and weaklings. I had received a letter from my mother saying she couldn't come to see me because that would mean leaving the others at home. Her lack of logic and inability to understand my loneliness was devastating. They had each other … I was alone. This episode confirmed my belief that she was incapable of loving me.

The last of the patients allowed out on leave had gone, and the room was empty. I had often wanted to be alone, but now I realized how much I hated it. The evening nurse came and pinned the emergency bell to my pillow. I knew the bell was for those who were very ill and I hated being considered sick.

"I don't need it, Karen, I'm not that sick."

"I know, but you'll be alone."

"I don't think the bell is very good company," I answered with a straight face.

"I know," she laughed, "but you are young and handsome, and you might need help."

This was the first time in my life anyone said that I was handsome.

"I don't know about the handsome part, but I do know that I don't need the bell."

"Oh, come on, Mickey, don't be so difficult. You're not alone on this floor. There are others who are staying. Some of these guys … well, some …"

"Some what?"

"Just wait a moment, and I'll get someone to explain it."

Karen was young and didn't know how to tell me about the dangers of being raped by another lonely patient or orderly. Being alone made me a perfect target. There were no security guards. Each floor had only one nurse for the evening, and one for the night shift.

A little later a hefty woman with red hair and freckles, who rolled her R's, came in and introduced herself as Miss McGregor. She sat on the edge of my bed and with kind words and a soft look in her eyes she told me about men who used young boys as if they were women and she went into more detail when she realized how little I knew. What she said sent shivers up my spine. I understood why Karen couldn't tell me.

I wrapped the bell cord tightly around my hand. The hours crept by. It was late in the evening when the door opened. Thinking of nothing else but homosexuals, I peeked out from under the blankets and held the bell firmly. To my delight it was Maggie. I had been so preoccupied I had almost forgotten that Karen' shift had ended and Maggie had started her rounds. She stood and looked at the empty beds, and smiled as she came closer. I moved aside to give her room. I had a feeling that something good was about to happen. It did. She kissed me, long and hard, like never before. It felt strange but good ... sinful ... joyful. Her lips were soft and warm, and I held and caressed her. It was all so very new. She pressed her lips firmly on mine, and I realized that she liked it as much as I did. That thought gave me courage, and

I boldly touched her breast. She gently pulled my hand away and smiled saying, "Wow, not so fast, Rome wasn't built in a day."

I realized I'd crossed the line but kissed her again, and then she left with a promise to come back later. I waited for her but later it was too late for me, she didn't return. The few patients that were left would be asleep, so I set out to find her. I went as far as the nurse's station and looked around. It was deserted, but a moment later I saw her come out of one of the rooms. When she was closer, I saw that she was crying. She told me that Mr. Featherstone had died. I didn't know him because he was in a private room at the other end of the hall, but I'd heard his name mentioned. He had been there many years, was well-liked and everyone knew he was very sick.

I would have wanted to take her in my arms to console her. I wanted to hold her and let her know that I understood how she felt even if I didn't, but I couldn't take that chance.

"I shouldn't care so much," she said as she blew her nose. "But I can't help it. It just seems so unfair, an old man dying alone like that."

I thought back to my father when on the train he had tried to give me reassurance. He had told me that tuberculosis was under control and hardly anybody ever died from it anymore. He hadn't looked at me, but he stared at the frosted window when he said it. I didn't believe him, as a matter of fact, I didn't think that he believed it himself.

I didn't say anything to Maggie; there was nothing to say

The next day started with a bang when Frank, an orderly, came in and shoved my bed hard against the wall. The beds had good wheels and rolled easily. They were moved back and forth between the rooms and the balcony every day. The orderlies couldn't do heavy work because they were ex-patients who had lost at least one of their lungs to surgery and they made sure that the beds' wheels were kept in top condition.

Frank was particularly fussy about having beds squarely lined up against the wall. He didn't have much else to feel important about. He seemed to take pleasure in giving the bed a good shove to let its occupant know that it wasn't lined up quite to snuff. It must have rolled away from the wall when Maggie and I were making out, and I'd forgotten to straighten it before I went to sleep.

I stayed under the covers and didn't eat breakfast. I wanted to dream a little longer about Maggie. Spam and eggs, toast and coffee, cornflakes or oatmeal that could have been mistaken for concrete, were the dietitian's favorite breakfast menus but not anyone else's.

I put my pillow over my head to muffle the sounds. It didn't take the girl who served breakfast long to report my fasting, and it wasn't long before Nurse Tang came over to see me. She put her hand on my forehead and looked concerned.

"What in the world is wrong, Mickey? You don't feel warm, but I'll take your temperature anyway."

"I'm fine, Nurse. I just didn't feel like eating spam and wet concrete for breakfast today. Given all the fuss ... I probably should have."

She left shaking her head but didn't try to change my mind. I wasn't the first to complain about the menu, and I wouldn't be the last.

Frank came back shortly afterward to put me out on the balcony but it wasn't one of my best days, and I proposed, "why don't you forget about me today?"

My plea fell on deaf ears.

"Look, boy, isse cold outsize, you put clothes, or I put bed out like dis."

I knew that he meant it, but I had hoped that Christmas Eve would bring some compassion. I heard the radio announcer say that the temperature was 30 degrees below zero.

At one point I dared to bring my head out from under the blankets and raised it high enough to look towards the road. I could see all the way down to the valley below. It was the middle of the morning and a long line of cars loaded with skiers inched along the narrow winding road towards the town. The newly fallen snow muffled the sound of the passing cars and the occasional honk of an impatient driver's horn. Regardless of the cold, I couldn't help being envious of the people out on the road and down in the village; they were free. The gray sky and white hillsides depressed me. Burying myself under the blankets, I pulled the black woolen toque over my ears and tried to sleep, but it was too cold. Frank came back a little earlier than usual and laughed when he saw I had crawled all the way under the covers. He poked me several times.

"Hey, boy, where you go? Isse you or isse pillow inne bed?"

Some patients would try anything not to be out on the balcony. They used pillows to give the illusion of someone in the bed and hide in the bathroom. The orderlies weren't fooled because as patients they had done the same thing themselves.

Frank had only one-half of one lung left. He wheezed, puffed and pulled up his shoulders with every breath. His caved-in chest made his belly look bloated and grotesque. He lived in a rooming house across the road from the San. Many ex-patients who lost as much of their lungs, as Frank had, also lost their wives. The lucky ones got a job at the San; it was the safest place for them to be.

I was out as usual for the afternoon cure. It was snowing, and the wind came up blowing a steady stream of powdery snow through the screening landing on the beds. I didn't dare to get out and push my bed inside. It was just too cold. In the meantime, Frank was ordered to bring everyone back inside, not out of compassion mind you, but the heavy woolen blankets stank when they got wet. Their dark brown color must have been chosen because it hid any dirt collected over the years. The bed linen was changed every week but not the blankets; it seemed they were never washed. When a patient died or was discharged the pillows, mattress and blankets were put out on the balcony to air out for a day. Blankets that got wet couldn't be folded and put on the bed as usual, so they were draped over the foot of the bed. They stank until they were dry and could be folded again.

The rain wasn't a problem because the beds could be pushed close to the balcony wall to stay dry. Light powdery snow, however, could blow right through the screen making the blankets smell like a musty old carpet on a damp basement floor.

It wasn't a busy shift for Frank, with most patients home for the holidays but he wheezed, huffed and puffed anyway. When he had finished his chores, he came back to visit me. He wheezed, and I tried to imagine trying breathing with only a quarter of my lungs.

I waited politely, as everyone did, for him to catch his breath.

"*Samela bitch*!" he said suddenly, slapping his knee. "*Now come dis fockink Silve Kink*!"

2

He walked down the hall bent over as if he were carrying a heavy load. His left arm was behind his back while his right swung back and forth. His face was wrinkled, his hair white and his bottom lip protruded and sagged, collecting spit that would come out as a spray when he spoke. Most people backed away from him when he talked but it wasn't always effective, he would follow matching every step to keep close to his victim.

Being confined to my bed made me especially vulnerable to a full dose of his liquid assets. The nurses saw him as a celebrity because he was a surviving crewmember of the Titanic. I was too young to care about his status. To me, he was a pest.

They called him Silver King. His real name was James Johnson. He'd worked as a steward on board the Titanic on the night it went down. I didn't believe it at the time, but I found out years later that he was indeed one of the survivors.

I recognized his photograph in a book entitled: *The Titanic Disaster,* by Dave Bryceson.

Silver King's story differed somewhat from what is written, but his photograph was unmistakable. Perhaps he had added some color or maybe his advancing years had taken their toll, but he told me in his own words what had happened.

James Johnson understood the urgency of the order to abandon ship. He watched several partly filled lifeboats being lowered and decided to get into one of them but was prevented by another crewmember who stood guard with a revolver. The situation continued to worsen, so he jumped overboard, petrified of being dragged down by the sinking ship. The black water was icy, but he managed to swim until he came to a lifeboat with a crewmember and some women. He was pulled on board and sat huddled on the floor while they drifted away.

Silver King stopped realizing that nothing else could possibly interest his skeptical audience. His face suddenly lit up, and he laughed out loud.

"God-damn it boy, I was almost a goner that time, but you can't keep an old bastard like me down for long."

As if the Titanic disaster weren't enough. He told me that he had experienced another shipwreck. He went down a second time when a U-boat torpedoed the ship he was serving on in the Second World War.

"Went right down with the goddamn ship, I did," he chuckled.

"Oh yeah … then how come you're here?" I taunted.

"Came right back up again, got hurt that time. They fished me out, and I passed out while they were hoisting me on board … don't remember much after that. The doctor told me they had to put a silver plate in my back to fix me up again. Still there, you want to feel?"

"No! No, I believe you."

I was afraid that the old man might get within spitting distance.

I didn't want Silver King to come to my room, but I couldn't do much about it until someone tipped me off on how to get rid of him. It was so easy, all I had to do was to ask him his age, and he would leave. He didn't want to think about it. By asking him, he was forced to face reality. He liked to pretend to be younger and talked about his girlfriend in Montreal as if she were young and obsessed with him. The fact was she never came to see him. He looked to be in his eighties, but even Nurse Tang said she didn't know how old he was. She probably did, but wouldn't tell.

One time I heard him shuffling towards my room. I crawled under the covers and pretended to be asleep. It wasn't long before he was at the foot of my bed, grabbed and shook it.

"Hey! Wake up young fellow; you're sleeping your life away!"

I stuck my head out from the blankets and looked at him.

He grinned and said, "God you're a good-looking one. You could have kept a sailor warm and comfortable as well as any good woman."

Embarrassed and angry I felt my face turn red as he

laughed out loud. He turned and faced the room as if he expected applause for his performance. He was the only one laughing and got no reaction because the others also tried to keep their distance from him. Nurse Tang must have heard him because she came in and asked him to leave. She looked furious.

It was Christmas Eve, and Frank left as soon as he heard Silver King. He shuffled his way past the door and alongside my bed. He looked around only to see the other empty beds. He was without an audience. I was prepared to ask him his age because I didn't feel very charitable.

He stood for a moment. The fact that there was no audience didn't seem to deter him, but I was saved by a knock on the door. Silver King's eyes lit up. He moved impatiently back and forth from one foot to the other. It had to be a stranger. Anyone else would have just barged in ... only strangers and new patients knocked. He looked expectantly at the door as the guest peeked in. I recognized the cassock. It took Silver King a few seconds before the visitor registered. Then he turned away and left in disgust. Apparently, there was nothing he hated more than a priest. I thought That I heard him say, "goddamn crow," as he went out the door.

The crow was a tall man. His gray hair was slicked back with grease.

"Good afternoon, son, I'm Father Dubois. I see from the records that you are a Roman Catholic. I thought that you might want to receive the Holy Sacrament on Christmas Day."

I was caught off guard, I'd always gone to church for that stuff but had never been visited by a priest. Not wanting to tell him that I was questioning the whole idea of religion, I decided on another approach.

"Father, under normal circumstances I would, but I'm in a state of sin, and I can't take Communion."

"Well, let's hear your confession, and after the absolution, you'll be in a state of grace again."

He reached for the chair and closed the door. I thought of Maggie and the sins I had committed. I wasn't sure if the way we kissed was a mortal or only a venial sin. Confession had always been from behind a little screen in a booth at the back of the church. To sit in the open, without the protection of a screen or curtain, and talk about my sins, was unthinkable. It was better to be in a state of sin and keep my self-respect.

"But, Father," I said, "I would have to be sorry for my sins, and I'm not. I will probably commit the same sins again."

The priest stroked his chin. It sounded like coarse sandpaper.

"If it is the sin I think you are referring to, prayer and meditation can overcome masturbation, and ..."

"No ... no, Father, that's not the sin I am talking about," I answered panic-stricken. "I'm just not ready for confession."

I could hardly tell him about my thoughts. I knew they were bad, I just didn't know at what point they were sinful. I couldn't sit there, look at him and confess how I had kissed Maggie and tried to get my hands on her boobs. It would have been more embarrassing than my first bed bath.

The priest put the chair back and looked me straight in the eye.

"I am sorry you've chosen the road of sin, but I will pray for you, and I hope you will see the light. In the meantime, let me bless you.

I couldn't very well object, and the priest blessed me before he I thought about the things I'd said, but I couldn't feel any different. It was the truth, and I didn't want to make my soul any blacker by lying to a priest. It was just about 7:30 that night when carolers from the village came to sing for the patients. After listening politely, I thanked them for thinking of me and said that I had no money to donate to their charitable cause. I felt stupid when one of them told me that *I* was one of their charitable causes. I had slept for a while that afternoon and didn't want to go to sleep when lights out was announced. I didn't want to chance missing Maggie after her rounds, but I fell asleep anyway only to be awakened by someone touching my shoulder. I jumped shouting, "Fuck off homos!" "Easy, Mickey, it's me, Maggie. I wasn't sure if you were sleeping.

"I wasn't," I lied. "I had my eyes closed and imagined being with you." She smiled warmly. Her uniform rustled with her every move. She sat on my bed, and we kissed. My hands wandered again, but she let me know the limits. I was glad that I hadn't confessed. It would have been a waste of time. Running my hand up her leg definitely had to be a mortal sin and according to my upbringing, anyone who died in this state went directly to hell!

Christmas morning came with a new layer of snow and a barrage of music. For most, it was a celebrated day. The daily announcement rescinded the usually enforced cure out on the balcony. Visitors were welcome throughout the day, but very few came. I thought of Christmas at home, and my throat tightened. It was late evening, and I decided to get up and move around a bit; I didn't want to stay in bed and feel sorry for myself.

Quite by accident, as I stood in the doorway, I happened to look towards the fire escape door where I saw a man standing outside in the snow. That door was a fire escape, and none could enter from the outside. I looked closer and saw that it was Henri Beaudry. How long had he been standing there? He didn't move. He was either frozen to death or just numb from the cold. Little puffs of his breath came out from his scarf, and he was apparently alive. Henry was used to the cold, he had been a lumberjack by trade and often used to work in the forest in the winter, but he had probably grown soft like the rest of the patients. He had been sick for a long time. Surgery had left him with only one lung, and his wife had divorced him. He went out on a pass once in a while, got drunk and bragged about his escapades the next day. The old-timers pretended to be jealous of his conquests, but they knew his chances of being with a woman were shot to hell the minute he displayed his caved-in chest with missing ribs and scars. It definitely wasn't much of a turn-on.

Henri had been given a day pass for Christmas; naturally, his drinking had made him forget the time. He could still have sneaked in by the front door, but that wasn't his usual way of getting back to his room. He had been known to stuff paper in the latch of the fire escape door and jimmy the alarm with a paper clip. He had probably forgotten to do it before he went out.

He stood leaning against the window with his head down. I hesitated. It wouldn't have mattered leaving him there if he were dead, but he was alive it would be criminal to leave him. His pitiful appearance was enough to break the rules. What the hell! I pushed the door open, and Henry stumbled in, dragging in a load of snow. The snow felt like stinging needles on my bare feet. The alarm was louder than I thought it would be. I saw Karen look around the corner of the nurses' station and I waved her away. She seemed to understand because she disappeared. Henri mumbled something while I steadied him. A fall would have made it impossible to get him up and to his room. His face was buried in his scarf, and he stank of beer and stale cigarette smoke. His wheezing and puffing were worse than usual. His climb up the fire escape had taken the last of his energy. He wanted to stop and rest as soon as he was inside, but I couldn't let him. I had to get him to his room, or we would both be in for a lecture.

The beer stench was overpowering but the occasional growl, whenever he hit the wall, was a sign that he still had some life left in him. He was heavy and started leaning more and more on my shoulder. I looked for Karen when we came to his room because it was directly across from the nurses' station, but I didn't see her. She had probably gone into Tang's office when I'd waved her away. Once we were in his room, I let him fall on his bed, and as he landed, he said with a stupefied grin. "hey ... old Mickey ... I fucked her! I fucked her good."

Karen came in. I went scarlet when I realized that she had heard him. I was embarrassed, but I should have known that she was used to situations like this. We grabbed his legs and lifted him all the way up on the bed. Looking at Henri, sprawled face down on the bed, Karen said, "Thanks, Mickey, it was nice of you to help him. I'll handle things from here. You better not tell anyone about this."

"But Karen, the way he is talking he ..."

"Oh, never mind, it's okay. I can handle him, it's not the first time."

I went back to my own room and stood by the balcony doors, thinking about Henri saying the word fuck, while she was putting him to bed. The wind drove the cold through the cracks of the old wooden doors, and I shivered. I saw Henri's trail crossing the snow-covered lawn. Drifts would soon cover it. I took my bathrobe off and went to bed. Christmas had come and gone. It was my first Christmas away from home. It had been sad and lonely, and I would not easily forget it.

It was about the time for Maggie to come on duty but Karen came in and smiled saying, "I wanted to tell you before I go off shift that you did a nice thing for Mr. Beaudry. He could have died out there if it hadn't been for you."

"Maybe he would have been better off."

"Don't talk like that; I know you don't mean it."

"Oh no? At least half the people here are long timers waiting to die. I often wonder if I will have a relapse after I leave here and be one of them."

"You're not like the others you're young, forget about that silly stuff."

She bent over and kissed my cheek just as Maggie came in. She looked upset, but Karen told her what I had done for Mr. Beaudry. I knew that Karen and Maggie were friends and they left the room together but only Karen smiled. Maggie came back after taking the shift and let me know how she felt.

"I don't expect any competition, and in future, Mickey Swager, you make it clear that you're not available."

She made me feel important by being jealous ... or pretending to be. She couldn't have been a better morale booster. But apparently, she felt that she should do something more to make me understand how she felt about me, because she came back later, without her cap. Her hair was long and loose. She looked very different. My heart was pounding as she came closer and went to lie beside me. We kissed and for a long time, and she didn't push my hands away when they wandered again.

"I love you, Mickey," she whispered.

"You're one hell of a man, Mickey Swager."

She kissed me holding my face in her hands.

It was the night I became a man, and I felt ten feet tall. When it was over, she smiled and said.

"I will always love you. Let nothing come between us."

A tear rolled down her cheek, and she didn't wipe it away.

"Did I hurt you ?"

"No, on the contrary, you made me very happy."

"Then why are you crying?"

"I cry because I'm happy. People don't always cry because

they are sad or hurt. Many people cry because they are happy. Now go to sleep, I want you to get well."

"Wait, Maggie. I guess I should have asked you this before, but in my excitement, I forgot."

"Forgot what?"

"Did ... did I give you the bug?"

"No, not likely. Don't worry about it."

"But the way we kissed and when I was inside you."

"Mickey, look, I was exposed to TB long before I ever saw you. Many people who are exposed never get sick. Take you for example. I know that you never kissed anyone the way we have, and you got sick anyway. It's highly unlikely that I'd get it from you. As a nurse, my exposure has probably given me more resistance to TB than other people. Don't try to scare me away because I won't let you go so easily."

3

Not the most co-operative patient in Nurse Tang's care, I was often lectured about not being in bed. My toilet privileges were an opportunity to get more freedom and linger for a while longer in the hall. There was a shortage of nurses willing to work in the sanatorium and patients weren't as closely monitored as they should have been. Silver King's visits must have given Nurse Tang the impression that I had a soft spot for the old men on the floor. Her need for my help with a problem became clear when she came with a proposal.

"Mickey my boy, I realize that my efforts to keep you in bed are failing. I'm not giving up, but we could legitimize the extra time you spend out of your bed."

"You mean you aren't going to give me any more lectures?"

"To a point, but it comes at a price."

"Damn! It sounded too good to be true. I should've known that you were going to have a BUT in there somewhere."

"There's no reason to swear ... are you listening?"

"Okay, I'm all ears!"

"Mr. Lewis loves to smoke, but we can't let him unless an orderly or nurse stays with him. He dozes off and sets fire to his bed. Sit with him for his after breakfast smoke each day, and I will occasionally look the other way. At least you'll be sitting rather than walking around."

"You're going to look the other way, but you're not going to make it legitimate or official?"

"Come on Mickey, you know I need Dr. Phelan's permission for that."

I stared at her for a moment and took pleasure in her dilemma. She must have mistaken it for contemplation and turned away expecting me to turn her down.

"Never mind, it was probably a bad idea from the start."

"Why?"

"I should have known that you would say no."

"I was going to say yes, Miss Tang."

"You were? I mean you are?"

"Yeah okay but only once a day."

"I'm so glad that you don't hold a grudge, Mickey."

"A grudge, for what?"

"The time that I gave you a bath and pretended that I was going to wash ..."

"Wash what?"

She blushed this time and walked away, but I felt good; I had gotten her to blush.

I kept my promise and took the job as Lewis' sitter. The first few days were spent in silence while he comfortably puffed away. At times, he looked suspiciously at me but always thanked me when he left his room. He didn't try to make conversation because he didn't expect me to come back. Like most patients, he didn't get many visitors. It seemed that the longer we were hospitalized, the easier it was for people to forget us. This old man was dying and in a private room where other patients seldom visited. Private rooms were for terminals, and like visitors, patients kept their distance. This made it easier when they were picked up at midnight and taken to the morgue. It wasn't an official rule but a silent one. I hadn't yet learned to turn my back, but I eventually caught on.

Most mornings Mr. Lewis would be reading his newspaper, but he would fold it and give it to me as soon as I entered the room. Nurse Tang was very strict about matches or cigarettes being too close to his paper because it would catch fire much quicker than bed linen. He broke the ice one day and actually spoke, offering to pay me for my time. He reached into his nightstand but stopped when I said that I didn't want anything for it. I could have used the money, but taking money from the dying old man just didn't seem right. After a few days, he came to expect my visits, because he would call out when he saw me in the hall.

The once dailies quickly grew to four. He was old, but by no means stupid or feeble-minded. Some of the staff believed it was easier to dismiss someone who was feeble-minded. As unacceptable and inhumane as it was, they theorized that an old man, who is nuts, can wait ... let him sit a little longer on the bedpan. The fact that he complained to staff that the newspaper people printed the same thing as the day before, did nothing to improve the staff's opinion of his mental status. I smiled when he started up with me. The staff was right; the old man was going nuts. Some said that in the end patients often went crazy because the TB bugs invaded the brain. I imagined those little buggers marching up the spinal column and feasting on the brain.

The doctor had shown me my own X-rays and pointed out the existing cavities in my lungs. The damn X-rays didn't mean squat to me, but If any holes were in my brain, I would be nuts for sure.

I took the burning cigarette from Lewis' hand and picked up the paper after he'd dozed off again. I looked at it and saw that it was two days old. The old man definitely did remember what he read, and he was entitled to his copy of his daily paper. From that day on, I went to the nurses' station early in the morning and picked up the paper before throwing the old one away. It was obvious that someone had been stealing his subscription. Lewis never again complained about it, his senility was miraculously cured.

It was a beautiful morning. The sun was shining, and it brightened every room. The temperature had gone up above zero for the first time in more than a week. I was ready to sit with the old man, but his door was closed with the "*do not disturb*" sign over his name. I waited but didn't hear anything from inside the room, so I went to see Nurse Tang. She came out of her office, and she hooked her arm through mine. She never did that, she was someone who would stand back and read someone's face. The way she acted told me that Lewis was gone. She told me that he had died that morning before breakfast. This was when I learned that a corpse lies in the room until midnight; seeing a corpse being moved to the morgue wasn't a morale booster for the patients.

"You want me to go in with you and say good-bye?" she asked.

I shook my head. She must have realized that she had written too much into my relationship with the old man. I felt a certain amount of pride when I could answer her without sounding emotional.

"No, he's dead; I don't want to look at a dead body."

She didn't seem surprised at my answer. Maybe she saw that I was drawing on some newly acquired coping skills, by adopting the same attitude as the others. She stood back and looked at me, but I wasn't about to let her read my internal feelings.

Father Dubois marched down the hall with a quick and determined pace. His shoes squeaked, and his cassock flopped around his legs. He didn't bother to acknowledge anyone. He had come to do God's work, but he was too late. His visit would have done more good while the old man was alive. This was the first time I had ever seen him go into Mr. Lewis' room. He let the old man die alone and wasn't there when he was needed most. The look on Nurse Tang's face told me how she felt about the priest. I'd never learned to lip-read, but I saw her say, "goddamn crow." She saw that I understood and smiled with. She was getting easier to read because I'd gotten to know her a little better. Her armored exterior was nothing more than a front to insulate her from the ugliness of the San. We shared a bond and age had nothing to do with it.

It was midnight, and I heard the clattering wheels of the empty gurney in the hall. Moments later those same wheels were almost silent under the weight of the corpse. I crawled under the blankets and shivered. I was scared and had no one to talk to. It wasn't as if we were friends. He had just become part of a routine that gave me some purpose, or at least that's what I tried to tell myself.

Maggie quit her job when we realized that we were in love. "Mount Sinai," the Jewish sanatorium on the other side of the village, was hiring and her experience was welcomed with open arms. She worked the night shift there and came to see me every day. We no longer had to hide our relationship, but we didn't enjoy the privacy we had while my roommates were away during the Christmas holidays. It was hard for me to be near her and only hold hands, but not seeing her would have been unbearable. Nurse Tang didn't look pleased when she saw that my most frequent and only visitor, was Maggie. It didn't take her long to put two and two together, but we didn't care.

It took another few weeks before I got the news that my condition was finally negative. "Negative," a magic word. I didn't need the dreaded strep injections after all. I was no longer a danger to society! I could kiss and make love as much as I wanted, without the fear of putting Maggie at risk. If only we had some place to be alone. Most of all I looked forward to moving down to the next floor, where there were fewer restrictions and a step closer to freedom.

My move came sooner than expected because my bed was needed for a new patient. Frank came in and told me to get my things ready for a move to the second floor. He didn't have to tell me twice. I threw everything on my bed. I would have liked to call Maggie with the good news, but I knew she had worked the night shift and would be asleep. She truly had become the center of my life. My thoughts, plans and everything else revolved around her. I had never dreamed that love was so all-consuming. The joy when I was with her, the loneliness when I wasn't and the fear of the possibility of losing her was overwhelming. She was six years my senior, but it didn't seem to matter to her even though I was so damned innocent. Perhaps that was the attraction in the first place. I wondered how long her fascination with me would last. She was someone I'd dreamed and fantasized about. She recognized and commented on qualities I didn't even know I had. She said that I should just take those compliments and accept them, but ... she didn't know how hard that was for me to do, given my background. It was inconceivable to me that someone actually liked me or better still, loved me.

Much to my disappointment, my new room was right across from another private room. I had thought that "the terminals" were only on the third floor. The patients on the second floor were closer to being discharged and looked forward to freedom. Why was it necessary to be reminded of how close we were to the same ill-fated private room?

The name on the door said "René Benoît." He was a stranger, and I preferred to leave it that way; I wasn't going to let René have any effect on my life. We both knew the score; the private room was the end of the line. I was getting more arrogant ... perhaps it was the fear of getting acquainted with someone only to lose him later. I wanted no part of anything that painful again.

The first Sunday after my move, I got up and got dressed. My jeans felt stiff after all the time I'd spent in PJs. I hoped to get out of the building but it was too cold, and the doctor wouldn't sign my pass. In my optimism, I'd overlooked the fact that I wouldn't have gotten a pass even if it had been the middle of summer. Just being on the second floor didn't necessarily give me the same privileges as some of the others. Maggie's daily visits were a breath of fresh air. She was a much better cure than any amount of fresh air out on the balcony. We walked the hall endlessly, holding hands. There wasn't any opportunity to make love, but the occasional kiss or touch was what helped me keep my sanity. We had made love often when my roommates were home for the holidays but the last time we were together had been New Year's Eve.

When I finally got the news about a weekend pass, I didn't tell my family, my memory of Christmas was still too fresh. I hadn't been important to them then, and they didn't matter to me now. If it hadn't been for Maggie, I would have tried to forget that day as I did with anything else unpleasant. She had turned my most difficult Christmas day into the most memorable night ever. I'd thought about going home but Maggie's suggestion of a weekend together was definitely a much better option. On the few occasions that my parents had visited, we were so uncomfortable around each other that I was as anxious for them to leave, as they were to go. Even though Maggie's idea sounded a bit shady, the possibilities were endless.

Maggie booked a cabin at a motel called, "The Whispering Pines." All I needed were some toiletries and the clothes I was wearing. With just the two of us, there was no need for anything else. Besides, I was used to sleeping in the raw before the san. I thought of nothing else once we made up our minds to spend the weekend together. Just thinking about being alone with her for the entire weekend, without interruptions and in complete privacy gave me goosebumps.

Maggie's face was aglow from the first moment I saw her. I threw my bag on the back seat of her VW and climbed in. The first thing I did was give her a long kiss and then put my hand under her sweater, but she pushed it away.

"Not here, Mickey, wait until we are in the motel, then I'm all yours."

She tried to look stern, but she couldn't help smiling when we drove away and said, "I think that I've created a monster."

"No, I always was one, according to my mother. Even so, how can wanting to make love to you be bad?"

"It isn't, and I love you with all my heart. As soon as we are alone, I'll show you how much I want you."

The motel was a five-minute drive down the road. A wooden sign showed the way. It was half hidden behind some branches; we would have missed it if we'd come after dark. The long driveway was partially overgrown and branches hitting the car were a sure sign that the driveway didn't get much traffic. I didn't expect too much concerning modern décor or utilities. Things brightened once we came to a clearing. There was a house with a tiny office but still no signs of life. I looked at the dozen or so cabins along the perimeter of the clearing. Most were badly in need of repair. Fewer than half seemed to be in good enough condition to rent out. The rest looked like they were used for storage or were being left to rot away. We went into the office where an elderly gentleman greeted Us. He reminded me of the character in Pinocchio, "Gepetto." His white, wavy hair needed a trim. His mustache covered his lips and probably got into his mouth when he ate. His glasses sat down on the bridge of his nose. The smell of fresh-brewed coffee and stale smoke came from behind a curtain separating the office from rest of the house. He scanned the page of the reservation book as if he were expecting many guests but there was only one name. He looked at us and said:

"You must be the Swagers."

I had a hard time not laughing. Maggie smiled while she filled out the registration card with Mr. & Mrs. M. Swager. The old man probably wasn't fooled by us trying to look as if we had been married for years. He had inevitably been in similar situations before. Maybe he was having just as hard a time containing his laughter. He looked at the board behind him for the key. Playing his role well, he pretended to have difficulty deciding where to put us.

"Cabin number 14 is for you folks," he finally said. "It should have been number 13, but most folks consider it an unlucky number, so we skipped it and went right on to 14," he chuckled as he put the key on the desk.

"That will be $26.00 for the two days ... uh, in advance that is."

He held out his bony hand, awaiting the payment. I put my hand into my pocket as if going for my wallet, but Maggie said, "it's okay dear, I've got it."

She knew that I had no money. She reached into her purse and gave Gepetto thirty dollars. He stared at the crisp new ten-dollar bills.

"I ... I'm sorry, ma'am," he apologized, "I haven't any change, you see I've just been to the bank with my deposit."

The old fox was a bad actor. He was hoping that she would tell him to keep the change. Maggie went back into her purse and with bits and pieces came up five cents short. I pretended not to hear any of it because I couldn't even come up with the missing nickel. I hadn't had any money in my pocket for weeks.

"That's all right ma'am, forget the nickel," said Gepetto generously.

Maggie thanked him and took the key. An old lady pulled the curtain back. Her hair was as white as his. She didn't appear to have any teeth but seemed to be chewing something. I watched her nose almost touch her chin each time she clamped her gums together, and I thought about the story of Hansel and Gretel and the witch

"Now don't give the store away, George," she squeaked. "Serves you right though. That will teach you not keeping enough change around."

She let the curtain fall back and continued to complain as she went back to the living quarters. Perhaps she was part of his act. The old man shrugged and raised his hands in resignation as if to say, *You see what I have to put up with!*

He walked us to the door and pointed to the cabin.

"It has no number," he laughed sarcastically, "the repair crew hasn't gotten around to it yet."

We drove across the clearing to where Gepetto had pointed. I looked back, and Gepetto waved. I wasn't sure why perhaps confirming we had the right place.

Once inside we were pleasantly surprised. Everything was old and well used, but it was as neat as a pin and clean. The bed was my priority; it was the whole reason for being here. Sitting on the edge, I watched her undressing. She knew how much I liked it and took her time. I stripped while she took the bedspread off and pulled back the covers. I was wild and desperate for her. It had been much too long, but we had the entire weekend, and I relaxed and took my time to get reacquainted with her body. I had never imagined that a woman could be so pleasurable. Each time we made love, I found something new to enjoy.

"I would have bought a ring and proposed, Maggie, but a diamond isn't in my budget."

"A ring isn't important; it's the commitment that counts."

I looked at the cheap tin ring on my finger. I once bought it because it was what boys did in my circles. My fingers were rather large; the months of force-feeding had made it a little tight. She watched me while I fought to get it off. After some soap and a couple of grunts, I finally managed. It lay in the palm of my hand and held it out to her.

"This is all that I have for now. Maybe when I get back to work, I can afford the real thing. Marry me, I will always love you and never leave you."

Her sobbing made it impossible for her to speak, but her tears confirmed her answer. She put her arms around me, and we kissed. She pulled a chain from around her neck, pulled it through the ring and put it back around her neck.

We left the motel on Sunday at noon and standing outside the cabin she said, "until the day I die I will think of this place with the best memories ever."

It sounded very romantic, but I knew that it would be a few years before he could fulfill my promise to marry her.

I sauntered back to my room engrossed in my thoughts and memories of the weekend. Her smell, soft skin, her touch and eyes that told more than words, her hair that ... I snapped back to the present realizing that I was near my room. Never wanting to flaunt my freedom I'd intended to be discreet and keep my weekend bag out of sight, but it was too late. There he was lying on his bed. He'd seen me returning from a weekend of freedom. I'd managed to keep from getting involved with René. It was common knowledge that he hadn't been outside in four years and here I was, a newcomer, walking around as if I would live forever. Late that night, I heard René cursing and asking God to get it over with. I'd heard him sometimes before, but irrationally or not I wrote it off as another "terminal's" deranged mind, I believed I deserved to hear him that night. It was God's punishment for my arrogance. I was tempted to go in and say how sorry he was for being such a shit but instead pulled the pillow over my head in an effort not to hear him. Guilt was the one thing I could not ignore.

Walking the hall the following day, I passed René's door

and nodded trying to break the ice and to see if it would be acknowledged. I couldn't just go in and say, "hi! I'm Mickey Swager. I've been ignoring you because you are dying.

The second time around he called, my nod had been enough. René's voice was loud and clear, having mastered the art of energy conservation by taking a few breaths, and then burst out short sentences.

"Hey, neighbor ... come in ... park your butt ... on the chair."

I introduced myself and shook his hand. There was nothing but skin and bone. René was so frail that I was afraid to squeeze. I remembered my father saying that a handshake had to be firm. It expressed honesty and strength of character. So I did my best to convey that message without hurting him. I didn't bother to explain not introducing myself the day we had become neighbors. I was sure that René already knew why. His youth startled me, but I managed to stifle the temptation to run. Only old people died. This was hitting too close to home. My discomfort may have been obvious, but René's need for companionship was even more so. The first topic of conversation was sports. It was blatantly clear that I knew very little about the subject, and I felt awkward, but I knew that René wanted to keep me there as long as he could. After a while, we discovered that we both liked to sketch and draw. We had a common bond ...

René told me that he had been diagnosed when he was twenty. Hearing that, I broke out in a cold sweat. René's first stretch was for a year after he was diagnosed. He spent another year at home recuperating, but a relapse put him back inside. Since then, it had all been downhill. Three surgeries left him with the lower lobe of the left lung; the rest was gone. He had roughly a quarter of his original breathing capacity. It was the end of the line. Pneumonia would be fatal. He had lived with TB for so many years that he had already given up on the idea of a normal life. How stupid of me to go in and see him. How stupid to think that it would do any good for either one of us. The remorse over my earlier behavior became part of my baggage. Upon my admittance, Nurse Tang promised to put me with patients closer to my own age. This was as close as I ever got, but I couldn't imagine that this was what she had meant.

In the weeks that followed René became as much a friend as possible considering our conditions. I was disgusted with myself for getting friendly with another patient, and a terminal one at that. René's future was never a topic of conversation. It was as if he knew how much I hated to talk about death. He had probably experienced the same fears when he was my age.

He became a little weaker each day, and it was apparent that he would soon die. During one of my visits he asked me to get a small box out of his locker, and when I opened the door, I saw that René had even fewer things than I did. I handed him the box and was about to leave when René said, "wait, Mickey ... I got this as a present ... but I could never use them ... My hands are too weak ... I want you to have them ... I'm dying and don't want ... them to be stolen ... It's important to me ... that you have them."

It was the first time that he had openly mentioned his

death. My first reaction was anger because it was the last thing I wanted to hear. It wasn't fair, and I hated him for it, even though I knew that I was the one being irrational. I accepted the box. It contained a dozen of the finest quality coloring pencils. They had never been sharpened. I stared at them, looking for the appropriate thing to say. It was the only thing of value that he owned, and he wanted me to have them. I graciously accepted them, but in doing so, I believed I was validating the acceptance of his death. He saw my reaction and tried to put me at ease.

"Look, Mickey ... don't make this ... a fucking drama ... It's a fucking box of pencils ... The fact that I am dying ... isn't a drama either ... I'm never gonna get out ... of this fucking bed ... and I'm tired ... You've gotta understand ... I wanna go."

"I can't understand. You've got a lot of time left. Maybe they will find another drug that works for you. Maybe ..."

René waved his hand impatiently.

"There is nothing left ... My ... lungs are cut away ... by the knife ... what's left is ... being eaten away ... by the fucking bug ... I don't have the strength to sit ... on the bed-pan anymore ... I'm wearing fucking diapers ... for Christ sakes ... I have never ... been in the sack ... with a broad ... No woman wants to ... sleep with a bag of bones ... I get as horny as you ... but the closest ... I get to sex ... is a bed-bath."

"You can't just give up."

"Fuck it, Mick I've ... spent ten years ... in this place ...

It's enough for me ... I prefer ... my heart stopping ... over pneumonia ... you've seen them ... guys going ... ain't you?"

He closed his eyes not waiting for another useless response. He was tired and wanted me to leave. He'd reached the end of his struggle and wanted to know that somebody cared. I thanked him and promised to put the pencils to good use. He smiled weakly without opening his eyes. Our conversation ended. We never mentioned the subject again. Two days later his door remained closed. The, "Do Not Disturb" sign was hanging over his name. Father Dubois was again absent.

That night, I waited for the sound of the gurney and heard the clattering wheels coming down the hall. René Benoît passed my door at ten minutes past midnight, May 29, 1958.

4

An old abandoned ski chalet stood on the same mountain ridge as the sanatorium. Built from heavy logs, the cabin stood solid. It had closed because bigger and better resorts had been built at the other end of the town. The main structure was still intact but weekend renovators had helped themselves to the interior walls, windows, and doors. Vandals had completed the job of turning the chalet into a useless shell. At dusk, it looked ghostly partly hidden by tall grass and weeds. Some of the patients, at least those well enough to be up-and-about, used it for a meeting place or the occasional romantic encounter. Patients seldom let their marital vows interfere with their sexual needs because to some, loneliness was worse than guilt. Without medical insurance or free, universal healthcare they were in effect, willingly or not, quarantined by the government. I had this confirmed to me in no uncertain terms, during one of my rebellious moments when I contemplated running away. I was unceremoniously warned that the police would see to it that my freedom would be short-lived. In fact, I was told I'd be lucky to reach the outskirts of town and to add insult to injury, as an immigrant, an attempted escape could lead to mine and my entire families' deportation. In other words, anything possible would be done to keep me from infecting the general public. I thought this was ridiculous. I was no longer infectious. But I was left no alternative but to accept their authority over me.

My relationship with Maggie was the only thing that made the restrictions less difficult to bear.

On a beautiful afternoon near the end of June, I took a stroll down the path to the chalet to meet Maggie. The narrow trail was flanked by Maple trees. Their branches created a long green tunnel. The chalet and the ski slope were at the end of the trail. Dressed in jeans and a T-shirt, I lazily strolled along and stopping to enjoy my reprieve from the smell of disinfectants, rubbing alcohol, and skinny bedridden patients. In the valley below, a lawn mower groaned as it chewed the rich, heavy grass. I took my time because as usual, I was early and assumed that as usual, Maggie would be late. The future seemed brighter than when I had first arrived at the San, and since meeting Maggie, I was determined to live the rest of my life with her. I often found myself thinking about the responsibilities of marriage. I was only 20 years old. It was strange how things had changed. The words "love and affection" had meant little until I met her. It wasn't something I had been raised to understand. Quite the opposite, a punch or a shove came easier than a kind deed or word. Love was something between my father and mother and ended there. Maggie had shown me how to love. She made me feel different, helping me to carry my baggage, easing the load.

Walking a little farther I heard arguing and shouting. I stopped, not wanting to run into any trouble. The shouting continued. It seemed to be coming from near the chalet. Kids did play there sometimes, but more usually in the winter when there was enough snow for tobogganing. I couldn't see anyone, but as I got closer, I heard a woman's voice. It was from Maggie! It sounded as if she were in trouble! I ran! I felt pain in my chest from the stress, but I didn't stop until I came to the chalet. Maggie and a man were struggling near the edge of the ravine behind the chalet. I yelled out: "Hey! Let go of her!"

He looked towards me, and I recognized Rodriguez, a South-American sailor who had been left at the port of Montreal, by the captain of a cargo ship because he was ill. The nurses at the San were scared of him and kept out of his way. He was infamous for his foul mouth and bullying tactics. The director of the San had unsuccessfully tried to get him transferred to another facility. He was now close to being discharged, much to everyone's relief.

He held Maggie's wrists, and she screamed, "he's trying to rape me!"

Rodriguez let go of one wrist and pointed at me, yelling, "get the fuck outa here and mind your own fucking business!"

Maggie took advantage of the distraction and managed to free her other hand and raced towards me. Rodriguez jumped after her. My first impulse was to take Maggie and run, but I knew that in my condition, I could never outrun him. There was no choice but to stand my ground. Big and very intimidating, the odds of coming out the winner weren't good. Sensing the need for a weapon, I picked up a piece of wood.

Maggie reached me and stood behind me as Rodriguez came charging at us. He was naked from the waist down, waving his arms wildly and yelling that he would tear me limb from limb. I felt my knees go weak and had visions of being slaughtered. When Rodriguez was at arm's length, I took a step sideways, holding the piece of wood over my shoulder like a baseball bat. I swung it at his knees. He dropped with a roar and grabbed his injured knee.

"You'll die for this, you fucking moron," he groaned. "I'll rip your heart out and piss on it."

I hoped he would give up, but the pain only made him angrier. He struggled to get up. He didn't want Maggie anymore; he was after me now. I had the upper hand as long as he couldn't get to his feet. But he managed to get up. Raising the wood over my head, I aimed for his shoulder and hit him as hard as I could. Rodriguez saw it coming and tried to avoid the blow by ducking. It landed on his neck instead. He fell forward with a grunt, twitched a few times and then lay still. I held on to my weapon, not sure that he would stay down. Maggie held my arm as we stood looking down at him. I felt myself shaking, but I didn't feel the pain in his chest anymore. I felt satisfaction at having beaten him. Maggie was safe.

"I think he's dead, Mickey, he's not breathing."

I prodded him, but he didn't move. I poked him again,

hard enough that if he had been alive, he would have responded. He couldn't be dead. Cautiously moving closer, I pulled the collar of his shirt back it revealed a blue swelling. Maggie knelt down and felt for a pulse, but couldn't find one. She turned his head sideways, his eyes were wide open. Shaking her head in disbelief, she confirmed my worst nightmare. "My God he's dead, you killed him. His neck is broken."

I stared at the body, I had actually killed someone. Being non-violent by nature, I had never even been in a real fight. My motto was, "run don't fight."

I couldn't go to the police; no one would believe that it was an accident. My stretch in the San made a lifetime in prison unthinkable. The only thing to do was hide the body.

We each took hold of a wrist and dragged the body to the edge of the ravine. We put his pants on him without realizing that it made no difference now how he looked. One push and he was over the edge. We heard branches breaking before he hit bottom with a thud.

"I'll have to go down and make sure that he's hidden, Maggie. It would be too dangerous to leave him in the open."

"Please be careful, Mickey. That wall is steep, and you're not in shape."

"I know, but it is the only way to get down there. I'll take my time and meet you in an hour at the sign of the township limits on the highway."

I watched her for a moment as she walked away. Then I started my descent. It wasn't easy, but the brush that grew along the wall gave me some foothold as well as something to hang on to. After a couple of scrapes, I reached the bottom not far from the body. The corpse was lying on its back, bent unnaturally. His dead eyes stared, and I was tempted to close them, but what was the point. I had to hide the body, and I discovered a hollowed-out area and started to drag him along. I needed to rest several times before I pulled him into the hollow. I couldn't stop shaking as I covered him with some rusty metal roofing, weighing the whole thing down with an old mattress and other junk. I took a moment to satisfy myself that nothing looked out of the ordinary and started to make my way along the bottom of the ravine. The brush was dense, and it took a long time but climbing back up the wall wasn't an option. Suddenly I found myself at the edge of the clearing, of the Whispering Pines Motel. Now I knew where I was. I circled around the clearing, and it only took a few more minutes to reach the highway. I walked to the sign and sat by the roadside to rest. I was sweating, but at least I had stopped shaking. It wasn't long before I heard the engine of Maggie's VW. She stopped, I got in, and we drove away. My mind was racing. I had been provoked. I had to protect Maggie and ultimately myself. Perhaps it was a mistake to hide the body and keep quiet. What if it were found and somebody else accused? Would I have enough courage to come forward and confess? How could I keep Maggie out of it? The more I thought about it, the more I was convinced I had done the right thing.

"I feel awful, Dan. It's all my fault. I wanted to surprise you by being early for a change, and while I was waiting, he showed up and started to grab me. I ran but without thinking headed towards the ravine. I was trapped. He held me by my hair while he took his pants off. I was terrified!"

"I think we should just stop talking about it and focus on behaving as if nothing has happened."

"You're awfully cool about this."

"No I'm not but what's done is done. There isn't anything we can do to change it. You know I didn't mean to kill him, but I had to protect you, and I had a right to defend myself. Let's be realistic."

"He'll be missed at bed-check tonight."

"Don't think I haven't thought about that. There is no reason to believe that we will be suspected of anything but just in case there are any questions we have to get our stories straight."

She nodded but seemed uncertain.

At the San, I kissed her cheek and went inside. She was more emotional than I, and she would have a hard time dealing with it.

The first thing I did was take a shower. It was still visiting time, and most patients were up and about. It was a blessing that Miss Tang wasn't the head nurse on the second floor; she read me too easily and would have known something was up. I didn't sleep much that night. I kept going over the events of the day to justify my actions. Every time I closed my eyes, I saw the dead man staring at me.

The next day Maggie came by. She appeared to have recovered to some extent but then to my horror I saw that her car was loaded with her belongings. What was she doing? She had to leave, she said. It was her way of dealing with it.

She would write to let me know where she would be. We'd have to put our plans on hold until she contacted me. She explained that she had dual citizenship and was moving to the US. She hoped it would distance her from the entire mess. I was beside myself and tried to convince her that it was safer to stay. Her sudden disappearance could be seen as suspicious. It was useless. She was so scared she was actually leaving me! Was she so selfish not to realize her decision would devastate me? Feeling numb, empty and betrayed all I could think of was "until death us do part."

Ironically it had but not in the way I could possibly have imagined. Watching her drive away, I was dazed by her behavior. She had left me. Deep down I should have known that this was where it ended, but I was too much in love to admit to it.

Henri Beaudry put me to bed that night. He didn't know why but sensed that I was upset about something. His own way of dealing with depression was alcohol and the hope of a willing woman. We went out through the fire escape. He took me to a bar and let me drink until I almost passed out.

No one ever questioned me, or anyone else as far as I knew, about Rodriguez' disappearance. It seemed everyone thought that he had finally made a run for it. The staff silently rejoiced and no one called the police, avoiding the possibility of his return. He was considered cured. Everyone knew that he knew no one outside of the San and he had nowhere to go but back to Montreal to wait for a ship.

With Maggie gone, I made myself a promise never to fall

in love again. I would never again let anyone get that close. My adult life began with Maggie. In a very short time, she had turned my world upside down. She'd made me feel like a man. She'd taught me not only about love but also about hurt and confusion. I just couldn't understand how she could leave me so easily after all we had gone through together. Not a day went by that I didn't think of her.

Conversely, not a day went by that I didn't fear the police arriving with a warrant for my arrest. Every day I waited for her letter, but eventually, I gave up hope. Sometimes I saw Nurse Tang. I was tempted to talk to her but decided it was better to keep quiet.

Almost a year after my arrival, I was discharged. I sat on the wooden bench outside the train station and ran my finger along the names carved into the weathered seat. Fallen leaves twirled in little cyclones driven by the autumn wind. Winter hadn't started, but it was cold. I could have returned home by bus, but I wanted to leave the way I had come. My philosophy was that perhaps, the year could become a vague illusion like it had never happened. One reality was that I had come as a frightened boy and I was leaving as a man but no less afraid.

I'd told no one of my discharge because saying goodbye was too final even though I knew her letter would never come. My future would be very uncertain for a long time. I was especially crushed when the doctor who discharged me said, "you'll never be cured of TB. The disease is arrested but not cured. The cavities in your lungs were very large, and some haven't closed, but they are calcified from the drugs you've been taking, it keeps the bacilli locked inside. You will have to be careful and look after yourself, or you'll be back with a relapse."

I asked him, apprehensively, when I could go back to work. The doctor was just like my father. He couldn't look at me but at the papers on his clipboard as he said, "you were a carpenter. But you'll never swing that hammer again. For the next year, you'll be recuperating and continuing the drug treatment, after that ... maybe a part-time desk job."

There was shelter inside the station, but I wanted to be outside to feel that freedom. The baggage handler preparing for the train's arrival gave me an occasional look while carried out his duties. The wind whistled through the bare branches and along the telegraph lines alongside the track. A coyote howled, and it was answered. The sky was gray and the landscape desolate. I wasn't quite as free as I wanted to be; I was going home because there was nowhere else to go. If I hadn't killed Rodriguez, I would have most likely been going home to Maggie ...

Someone was coming up the steps. To my surprise, I saw Nurse Tang stepping up to the platform. I stood up. She looked frail and small in these different surroundings. Her scarf was loosely wrapped around her graying hair. She must have been beautiful when she was young. Her dark eyes had a softness; it sure wasn't the way I saw her when we first met. Had I changed or had she? She hesitated. A moment later she approached and stood beside me.

"Left without a goodbye?"

I felt awkward. I should have made her the exception and

taken the time to say good-bye. I felt bad because she had extended her friendship and cared for me.

Without another word, she slipped her arm through mine. The wind brought the first snowflakes, and with it, the memory of my arrival flashed back like the cold of winter. I felt lost and scared, tears were close but ... I knew the rules.

"It's been a very hard year for you, Mickey."

"Yeah, Victoria, it must admit it has been a bitch of a year ..."

"So, who gave you permission to call me by my first name?"

"You, when you decided to see me off. I know I should have taken the time to say goodbye; I know I was wrong. I'm glad that you came; you're like a friend. I wouldn't have wanted anyone else here. Today is my first day of freedom. It should be special, but it doesn't feel that way."

"I'm glad that your lungs healed so well, Mickey, but your heart will take a lot longer. I was afraid for you. You weren't like the others in there ... you should never have been in that place, you were too young and so innocent. You learned some hard lessons."

She turned and looked up the hill.

"In there, people grow indifferent, even bitter. For them, it's the way to survive. You have quietly built walls around yourself, but they'll come down some day. I know that Maggie hurt you, but try not to judge her too harshly. You're a fine person, and I hope that my own daughter will meet a man exactly like you someday. Go home and start again.

You're still young, you're 21, and you have the time to adjust and take stock."

"Does that gnawing pain inside ever go away?"

"Perhaps eventually, but there isn't any pill to help. You have to fight that battle alone. Please don't let your anger destroy the good things that are still to come. I'll keep an eye on you from time to time, to see how you are doing."

"I hope not. I want to forget all this as soon as possible."

"Understandably but I feel a bond with you, and I'll keep an eye out, whether you like it or not."

"Some things you say don't make much sense to me but maybe they will when I've lived a little longer."

We heard the rumble of the oncoming train.

"Come and give me a hug before you go. Who knows, we may meet someday again when times are better."

"You've got to be kidding, a hug?"

She smiled, "Yeah a hug, don't worry, unlike TB, old age isn't contagious."

I put my arms around her. She was frail, not at all like the tough woman she pretended to be. She held on to me, and when she let go, she took a tissue from her purse and wiped her tears. She wasn't sad because she was smiling. I was curious but didn't question her. It was hard to believe that I would never see her again.

"I know how hard that was for you, Mickey, and that makes it all the more special."

She walked away, down the steps and up the hill, turned once to look back, but she didn't wave. I boarded the train with the smell of disinfectant on my clothes and my little bag as empty as it had been when I arrived. I was going home, and as much as I wanted all of this to be an illusion, the reality of the year would be with me forever. I closed my eyes, and with the motion of the rocking train, my head started to bob ...

5

After looking up at the canopy of lush foliage, I looked around the perimeter of the open space surrounding me. Dew made spider-webs look like tatted doilies on chairs in a Victorian parlor. I listened to the chattering monkeys, screeching macaws and rustling leaves while inhaling the damp air and the musty odor of decaying vegetation so distinctive to the rainforest; it was a good day to be alive.

Other than my blond hair and blue eyes, I seemed to blend in with the local population. My drab clothing and tanned skin allowed me the freedom in this remote village to come and go without being a curiosity. I'd been coming several times a year for the past eight years, always admiring the beauty surrounding me. The unchecked boundaries of indiscriminate logging had done much damage to the forest. I knew that I was also to blame for the devastation but justified it by reasoning that I was "selectively harvesting." Besides, this was my living, as it was for Juan Hernandez, the local logger who was unconcerned about the loss of forests.

It was his country, yet he felt my operating methods were skewed too far to the preservation side of the balance sheet. I chose the trees I wanted and identified them with a bright orange spray paint, but whenever I passed through to the same places I'd been before, I saw how they had continued felling trees that should have been left standing. It created voids unsuitable for new growth. In the past, some of the locals had tried to use the open areas for farming, but neither the soil nor the climatic conditions were suitable for crops or livestock, and the land was eventually abandoned.

In spite of my stance on preservation, at times a log on the list of endangered species was mixed in with the regular logs, by choice rather than error. The fact that I needed the lumber, and Juan the money, made us allies in this lucrative enterprise. Whenever I saw Juan's little house, with the added room that served as an office and a drunk tank, I thought back to my lean years, after my stay in the sanatorium. The difference between Juan and me was that I lived in a country of opportunity, having earned enough to retire while Juan seemed to be struggling just to make ends meet. True, his standard of living was far above others living in his village, but that wasn't saying much.

My Land Rover was parked about a mile back, where the dirt road narrowed down to a trail, and large roots crossed the surface. In places where the ground was soft, trucks had made deep ruts, rain turned them into muddy ditches, but it was the only way into the forest. Trucks that came to pick up logs often brought rocks and other debris to fill the deepest ruts, but new ones always appeared after the rains. A trucker desperate to get out of a bog sometimes used a chainsaw or ax foraging for wood to get traction.

I preferred walking an extra mile or so, rather than bounce around, or risk being bogged down.

As I hiked on, I heard a child crying, and I stopped. I was quite familiar with the forest, and this sound didn't belong. There wasn't anyone working to fill the ruts, and I didn't hear any chainsaws ... Something was very wrong. It was too far from the village for children to be playing and being a school day made checking it out it a priority. The crying seemed to be coming from somewhere away from the trail. I spotted a Jeep a couple of hundred yards ahead parked between the trees partly hidden by the underbrush. Dropping my backpack, I was about to go over and investigate when a snake crossed my path. Not crazy about them, I kept my distance. The snake was in no hurry and showed no interest in me, as it slithered into the brush. By the time I reached the Jeep, the crying suddenly stopped, but I heard movement from behind the brush. I parted the branches and stepped into a small clearing. A few yards away, a man was bent over pulling up his pants. Beside him lay a child, face down. There was also a neatly folded jacket, with a holstered gun lying on top of it. It was clear to me what had taken place. Startled by my sudden appearance he looked bewildered, but quickly recovered shifting his eyes from me to the jacket. Dropping his pants, he made a dive for it but tripped over his pants and fell a couple of feet short. I snatched up the gun, cocked it and aimed it at him. Frustrated he cursed smashing his fist angrily on the ground. He got up, reached down for his pants, but I fired a shot next to his feet.

"Hey, are you out of your fucking mind" he barked. "You could've hit me. I just want to pull my pants up."

"Don't bother scumbag or the next shot will draw blood."

He stood still while I moved cautiously towards the child. Keeping the gun pointed straight at him, I knelt down and felt for a pulse, but the child was dead. A sizeable bloody mess on the back of the head was evidence of the murder. The rock he'd used was lying beside the body. I looked at the killer who laughed nervously.

"I would have left you some if I'd known you were coming. People out here don't care much about these kids anyway. They have far more than they can afford."

"So, this is your way of dealing with overpopulation you piece of crap ... Who the hell are you anyway?"

He didn't answer and avoided looking at me. Being in this remote area would make it almost impossible to hand him over to the authorities. There was always Juan's drunk-tank, but it was unsuitable. It wasn't usually locked. Overnight guests checked themselves out once they had sobered up. The city, on the other hand, was a two-day drive. To try to drive and watch him was equally as unlikely as letting my prisoner drive at gunpoint. The slightest distraction would give him the chance to overpower me. Tall and muscular, he was too strong for me to come out the winner. Ignoring what he had done was unacceptable. There had to be a way to keep him secure. Shooting him in a kneecap was an option. I picked up the jacket to look for identification, but a pair of handcuffs fell out. Could he be a cop?

I ordered him to a tree. At first, he was defiant, but I fired a convincing round, narrowly missing his head.

"You'd better do as I say or the next one will be in your ugly skull," I warned. "I would love for you to give me an excuse."

"Okay, just let me pull up my pants, or I'll trip."

"Leave'm down and get your ass against the tree."

He inched back. I threw him the cuffs but he made no attempt to catch them, and they fell in front of his feet.

"Pick 'em up and cuff yourself against the tree or you'll never walk again."

"Yeah, right. As soon as I bend down you plug me."

"No need to wait for that I can plug you now."

"What are you, some kind of faggot?"

"End of discussion! Do it."

He picked them up and did as he was told without another word. Keeping a safe distance, I checked that he was secure, standing in front of him I asked, "who the hell are you?"

He didn't answer and tried to stare me down. I drove my fist into his stomach as hard as I could. He roared. Bent over he drooled, gasping for air. I went over to the child's body and turned it over. It was a girl about 10 or 11 years old. Her face was bruised, scratched. Pieces of moss stuck to her drying tears, but she was still clutching a candy bar in her hand. Her head had left a deep impression in the damp moss, and it was evident that he had raped her. Feeling sick, I picked up the jacket again and continued to search through the pockets.

Along with his wallet, I found some money and his I.D. He was what I suspected, a cop, Geoffrey Savoy, working for the DEA. In another pocket were some stubs, receipts, notes and a photograph of me.

"What the hell is this?" I asked astounded.

He didn't answer but stood looking at me with his mouth hanging open, still drooling from the blow. The picture was recent, but there was nothing in the background to indicate where it had been taken. I asked again threatening to kick him in his groin, but he grunted, "you're fucking with the wrong guy. I'm not alone, I've got friends here. You can't hold me."

"Yeah ... I know I can't hold you, you piece of crap, but I can pull the trigger and blow your brains out. After that, friends won't matter."

"You pull that trigger, and my buddies will be here in a flash."

"I've fired twice, and nobody showed up; a third time will make no difference. Either your buddies don't care or want nothing to do with you. Tell me why you have my picture. I'll find out eventually so you might as well tell me. I can afford to be here as long as it takes. Save yourself some unpleasantness."

Savoy didn't answer and after another couple of good punches left him gasping for air without any results, I knew that threats or pain weren't enough to make him talk. I needed help and a witness. There was only one person close enough whom I could trust.

I put Savoy's jacket over the girl and checked the

handcuffs once more. When I started to leave Savoy yelled, "for Christ-sake ... Swager! Don't leave me here like this."

"Okay ... you not only have my picture but my name. You know more about me than I do about you. Be smart, tell me what's going on or it will get very unpleasant for you."

"If you leave me here I might not be alive when you get back. This is a dangerous jungle, the wild animals ..."

"Yeah, that bothers me a whole hell of a lot ... I'll bet that the only animal here is you, you pond-scum."

"Jesus, can't we make ... sort of ... a deal?"

"A deal, what deal?"

"Cut me loose, and I'll tell you everything you wanna know about your picture and why I'm here, and you'll know exactly where you're at."

"Exactly you said. You mean I listen to your story, then I forget about what happened here, and I let you go?"

"Yeah ... yeah, like ... I'll get rid of the kid. Kids get lost here all the time. I even read once of one being swallowed by one of them big snakes. They'll think that she got lost in the jungle or something ..."

"Yeah ... okay ... sounds good to me. You've got a deal. Talk!"

"Uh, uh ... first cut me loose and then I'll talk."

"Go to hell you son-of-a-bitch. How stupid do you think I am? I'm going to get help, and I'll make you talk."

Savoy grunted and groaned, fighting against the handcuffs, he was still cursing me after I disappeared into the jungle.

Juan looked surprised to see me. Inspecting and marking

the trees that I wanted should have taken all day. We hadn't planned to meet until later that evening. I told him what had happened. He didn't say anything but spat on the ground and looked towards the tool-shed where he kept a shotgun, but he saw the gun stuck in my belt and shook his head.

"I no need my gan for samelabitch, you gan iz enough."

"It isn't mine; I took it from the guy."

"Iz okay Mickey. You gan, hiz gan, is okay for me. Diz gan have bullet yez?"

"Yes, plenty."

He climbed into the driver's seat of the Rover as if it were his own. I didn't mind and gave him the keys because he would get back to the clearing faster. He and his men had cut the trail, and there was less likelihood of him to getting stuck in the ruts

The normally talkative Brazilian was silent. He stared straight ahead. His dark skin and unshaven sweaty face made him look mean and angry. The child was most likely from his village. It wouldn't have mattered any less if she weren't, but it is a lot harder to bring bad news to a neighbor than to a stranger.

It was evident that Savoy had tried everything to get loose. His wrists were grazed and bleeding. Juan barely acknowledged him and went straight to the jacket and lifted it. He recognized her. He stood for a moment looking down at her and then he swore. He shook with anger and clenching his fists he roared at the sky.

Give me de gan!" he demanded.

His black eyes sparked through now narrow slits. I was

afraid he'd kill Savoy before we had a chance to interrogate him. He was short-tempered, I had to stall him. I took the picture out of my pocket, but he ignored it.

"Goddamn give me diz fockin' gan!"

"Jesus! Juan ... We can kill him later, listen to me, please."

"I no kill later, I kill bastard now. He live more one minute, iz too lonk."

"You're the *law* around here. At least listen for a minute and look at the damn picture. I have to know why he has it."

Angrily he cleared his throat and spat a huge gob. It landed on a branch beside him and slowly sagged to the ground. It gave him a moment to think.

"Okay, I look, and I listen after I kill samelabitch."

I showed him the picture and explained how I'd found it in Savoy's jacket, stressing the importance of finding out why. Juan calmed down. Taking the bandanna from around his neck, he calmly wiped the sweat from his face and inside his hatband and spat another gob.

"Yez, you right, Daniel," he agreed, *"you don't got no info-mation, you never gonna be safe no place. Diz man have to kill you because you see diz,"* he said pointing at the body. *"You witness now."*

"I know. I have tried everything to get him to tell me, but he won't talk; this bastard can handle pain."

"Wait in diz place; I come back in little time to make thiz bastard tell you. I make promise to you, he tell to you everyting he know."

Not waiting for an answer he went into the jungle. As the Mayor, Police and Town Clerk of the village, he expected to be obeyed, so I did. Savoy didn't speak, but his eyes didn't seem to miss a thing. He tried to take full advantage of the fact that Juan was gone.

"The fucking greaser left ya, for Christ sakes. He's gone you ass-hole. He don't want to have nothing to do with this. He knows damn well that us guys from the DEA stick together."

I ignored him. His situation was desperate enough to try anything to get free. One thing was sure if he got loose one of us would be dead. He wasn't bluffing about the DEA guys sticking together. Even if I were successful in turning him in, without evidence, it would be his word against mine, and his organization would back him up. I had no alternative after I had my information I would hand the gun over to Juan.

I breathed a sigh of relief when Juan came back until he saw the huge snake he had firmly gripped behind its head. Juan grinned and stuck the snake's head almost in Savoy's face. The tongue almost touched him as it flipped in and out. Savoy whimpered. I approached cautiously, but Juan assured me it was safe. Regardless of the tragedy, he seemed to enjoy instilling fear. His eyes glittered feverishly as he held the snake's open mouth within inches of Savoy's groin. The sight was enough to make me cringe. Savoy turned white and started to shake. I asked him again, "what are you doing here?"

"I'm on a contract. I ... I came to blow you away."

"Me? What the hell for?"

"I dunno. I just came for the hit, that's all."

"Who wants me dead?"

"I dunno. I … I never saw the guy."

"Now that makes a lot of sense. To sum it up, you travel all the way to Brazil, to kill a man you don't know, for a client you don't know, and the only reason is the money?"

He didn't respond and kept watching the snake as Juan brought it closer. No longer able to remain silent as the snake was ready to strike, he screeched, "for fuck sake, please! Okay, okay! McBain … James McBain."

"Who the hell is McBain?"

"I dunno … He's some fat fuck politician in Washington … a senator."

"Never heard of him. Why does he want me dead?"

"I dunno. People like him have their own way of dealing with political problems. He didn't tell me. All I know is that he wants you wiped out and he don't want it done at home. I got to do it here and make sure that nobody ever finds you."

"What am I worth?"

"What kind of fucking question is that?"

"Let's put it this way. How much is he paying you for killing me?"

"Fifteen big ones. Five before and ten after."

"Why? He must have given you some reason."

"Why-why-why, fuck how the hell would I know. I got an extra five up front. I usually get ten for the job. He didn't want me to ask no questions, and he wanted me to do it alone. Because he said, that he didn't want me to leave any loose ends. He didn't want you back, not even in a box. He said he'd be watching."

Juan brought the snake closer again, and the serpent opened its mouth wide.

"For fuck sake man!" He screamed pulling himself tightly against the tree. "I don't know why! It's the truth. I swear to God. Please, don't let him. I told you everything I know."

I wasn't sure that he'd told me everything, but I knew enough.

"That's it, Juan. I know enough."

Juan paused for a few seconds, the temptation in his eyes was there, but he walked to the edge of the clearing and threw the snake back into the bushes.

"Why did you let it go? I could have shot it. Tomorrow the damn thing might bite someone."

Juan shrugged and watched it slither away.

"No ... not him. Diz snake have no poison teeth; he only bite to eat little animal for food. He scared, never bite no people only little mouses and birds."

"But his mouth was wide open; he was ready to bite when you held him close."

"Oh..no ... that old trick my father learn me. I squeeze one place, and he canno help open his mouth."

Juan was serious again.

"Give me gan now, diz man must die. I no ask you as Juan Hernandez, I ask as friend, give me diz focking gan.

"No, Juan it is because you are my friend that I have to do it. He came here to kill me, and I will shoot him. You can help. Bury him and get rid of the evidence.

"You kill before?" he asked with amazement.

"Once, a long time ago."

Juan nodded. *"Okay, you shoot samelabitch."*

Savoy heard every word and shrieked. There didn't seem to be any conflict over killing the man in cold blood, not when I looked again at the little girl's body. I knew what I had to do. In most US states, Savoy would have gotten the death penalty for this anyway. No doubt, McBain would send others to take his place, but at least there would be one less and give me some time to find out about the Senator.

"You're gonna fucking do it; you're gonna fucking blow me away" He screamed in disbelief as he frantically jerked against his restraints.

"Isn't that what you were going to do to me? An eye for an eye, bastard!"

"Well ... I told McBain that I would, but I wasn't really going to."

"Oh, sure you dumb ... lying bastard. I'm sure as hell going to blow you away ... ass-hole. Besides you're already dead anyway. Just think; a US senator hires you as a killer. Do you think that he's going to let you walk around with that shit in your head? He doesn't want to leave any holes, remember? How can you be so stupid? He'll pay you for the job with a slug in your brain the minute you get back home. You're history whether you do the job or not.

Savoy bargained, "look, Swager, I can make sure that nothing will happen to you. I can arrange for a new identity. We do it all the time for witnesses."

"Yeah ... yeah ... yeah, sure ... everybody knows about that trick. I wonder how many of those witnesses wind up with their new identity on a headstone, after all, it is more economical and permanent.You know as well as I do that the DEA has its own rules and is apparently accountable to no one. You guys don't even need presidential approval to kill somebody as long as you don't do it in your own country."

I could see the wheels in his head turning, but he didn't answer, he understood that my decision was final. Even if I didn't shoot him, Juan would. I stood in the middle of the clearing, about to disrupt the peace of the forest.

Juan looked on and didn't rush me but still curious about my admission of having killed before he asked, *"when you kill before it was like diz, with gan?"*

"No. It was an accident. I broke a man's neck in a fight. This time I do it because I want to respect myself, which I couldn't do if I let you do the dirty work for me."

I looked at the monster against the tree and cursed him, "damn you Savoy, God-damn you! How dare you put me through this." Stepping forward I tried to force the gun into his mouth, but he clenched his teeth and struggled, shaking his head from side to side, frantically trying to keep the gun out of his mouth. His lips were bleeding, and his eyes widened, it looked as if they were going to pop out. It had to be his mouth. I wanted to fire only once and be sure that he was dead; I didn't know if I had the stomach to shoot twice. I once read that a shot in the head any other way is not always fatal. I brushed the wet sticky hair away from his eyes with the end of the gun-barrel, wanting to see his eyes at the moment of death. Holding his chin, I forced his jaw down and pushed the muzzle roughly into his mouth. Savoy lifted his head and his face contorted as he closed his eyes.

I pulled the trigger. His head snapped back against the tree as the shot echoed through the forest bringing instantaneous panic. The monkeys screamed; the birds flapped their wings, screeching in terror and surprise.

Savoy's head fell forward, and the corpse sagged down as its bladder emptied. I dropped the gun and looked down at him. A large hole showed how the bullet had blown away part of his skull and taken most of the brain along with it. The surrounding bushes and trees were splattered with blood, brains and bone fragments, so was I and I wiped my face with the sleeve of my shirt. Blood trickled down along his hair and dripped to the ground where the moss soaked it up. I had violated my most favorite place in the world. The stench of cordite and death mixed with the jungle air and the musty smell of the fungus on the decomposing vegetation.

As quickly as panic had arisen, it calmed. Peace quickly returned for the birds and monkeys but for me, it never would again. I felt sick and steadied myself against a tree as my stomach churned in disgust.

I turned my back on the corpse. Juan took the little girl's body, wrapped it in Savoy's jacket, and carried her away. I took one last look at the man I'd just killed. I should have felt relief but didn't. Remembering the guilt over the first man I killed fifteen years earlier, I thought that perhaps I had something in common with a soldier; killing became easier each time I took a life. Regardless of having read that every time a man kills someone he dies a little, I felt very much alive.

Juan kept walking until he reached the Rover. He held her tenderly while I bounced the jeep along the trail. We stopped at a small house in the village. Chickens scurried out of harm's way as a woman armed with a broom, chased a squealing pig out the door. Juan carried the little girl in as the woman watched in horror. She dropped the broom, grasped her breasts, and screamed a bone-chilling cry.

Back in my room, I poured water into the basin and washed my face and arms. I took my bloodstained clothes and burned them in the fire-pit behind the house. I saw the villagers who ambled along the dusty road and gathered in little groups to talk about the child's death. I didn't sleep that night.

Early the next morning Juan came over. There was sadness in his eyes. My departure had always been a cause for celebration because of the deposit for the logs and the prospect of the balance, once the cargo was in the hold of a ship. But not this day; he looked stern, shaking my hand and looking into my eyes he said.

"Adeus meu Amigo, an never come back here Mickey."

He was letting me know that he too felt the overwhelming weight that had come upon our relationship. Juan dispensed his own brand of justice. He made sure that any crime in his village was dealt with the way he felt was just. It wasn't always according to Brazilian law, but his methods obviously worked because until now his village had no history of violent crime until I brought it there.

I arrived in the city late in the afternoon, after two days on the road. I took a room at a hotel and arranged for the return of the Rover. My next priority was a shower. I hadn't had one since I'd left the city six days earlier. Still sensing the blood and brain all over my body, I scrubbed until my skin was raw. Dried blood in my hair mixed with the water and ran down my chest. While washing my hair I felt something hard and sharp, and I picked it was a bone fragment, and I shivered. Finally satisfied that I was clean, I sat on the tiny balcony. The small cast-iron chair was uncomfortable, but the air felt good on my bare skin. I savored my drink while looking out over the rooftops of the shantytown along the riverbank and at the houses of the more affluent on the hillside. The setting sun tinted the polluted air over the city to an orange haze. Yet, in spite of the pollution, the squalor, the heat, and coarseness of the environment, I realized how much I loved Brazil and how much I hated Savoy for taking it away from me. Even if I had known the heavy price awaiting me, my decision would not have been different.

6

With the attempt on my life in Brazil occupying my thoughts, I stood by the window and saw Joanne drive into the parking lot, as the last snow was being cleared away. She slammed the car door shut, looked up to the window and waved. Minutes later, she burst in with an armload of mail.

"Heyaaa ..., Mickey, how are you doing this rotten morning?"

"Rotten like everyone else in this weather."

"You're back early. I didn't expect you until next week. What happened?"

"Oh ... ran into a little problem. There won't be any more shipments from Brazil, at least not for a while."

"Why not?" she asked astounded? I have customers waiting for some of that rosewood."

It's complicated."

"Complicated how?"

"Legal problems; it's better if you don't know."

"Finally got caught with some of those logs on the hot list, didn't you?"

"Let's not get into it just now."

"Okay boss."

She was mulling it over probably trying to find a solution to appease the instrument makers waiting for the exotic woods.

"You're still driving the clunker, I see."

"Hey, I don't make fun of what you drive. Come to think of it, why would I, a four-wheel drive at this time a year would be great."

"Well, get one."

She didn't answer or even look at me, but she started sorting the mail. Her blond hair fell forward so I couldn't see her expression, but I had known her long enough to sense that something wasn't right. I didn't want to pry, but since her mood had so suddenly changed, I realized that I had said something wrong.

"Did I say something to piss you off?"

"You could say that."

"What ... what did I say?"

She turned looking almost angry standing with one hand on her hip, the other leaning on the desk as her blue eyes stared intently at me. She was a woman who could look at someone that way without blinking for the longest time.

"Simple, look at the price of new cars and the stub of my paycheck, and you have your answer. You aren't here most of the time and life goes on. Prices are rising, and the value of the dollar is less all the time."

"So, you want a raise is that it?"

"Yes, among other things. I wasn't going to mention it since you just came home, but I guess this is as good a time as any. It isn't that I want a raise, I need it!"

"How the hell am I supposed to know if you don't tell me, shit ... I don't even know how much you earn?"

"God almighty ... I knew that it was going to be one of those days when I got up this morning. Get real. We work for you. We don't own the place. If you cared enough, we wouldn't have to ask. You would take more interest in the people that work for you. If you valued me, I wouldn't have to ask!"

"Jo, we're friends for Christ sake?"

"Even more reason, I shouldn't have to ask!"

I had been so busy expanding my supplier lists that I ignored the other aspects of running the lumber import business. Joanne was one of the most competent and hardworking employee; I could not afford to lose her. She was actually more like a partner.

"Yeah ... You're right ... I have been a bit of putz."

"A bit ... that's a hell of an understatement!"

"I guess I've got to make some changes."

"If you want to keep those two girls out front you do."

"And you?"

"Well, I'm not getting any younger, and I don't have a pension. That has started me thinking lately."

"Let's go for coffee and talk. I've got an idea."

"No, I don't want to go out now that I'm warm, talk here if you want."

"Yeah okay, look I've got an idea. Raises are no problem and I do have an idea for your pension plan. You've been handling all the domestic stuff. Sales are way up. There's plenty of money. We have no yards, no trucks, or anything like that to worry about. You don't really need me, the whole business is run from here, and I like it that way."

"Yeah, tell me about it."

"Well ... maybe ... you should pay yourself from now on."

"Are you firing me?"

"No, don't even think about leaving. I'll slice the tires on the clunker and chain the door to keep you. No ... I was thinking if we were partners, you could share in the profits. Leave your share to build equity or invest it in a pension plan, do whatever you want. The raise is fine, but I want you to have more."

She became more relaxed, and the harshness left her face as she began to blink normally.

"Cute, but what do I have to do for it. You wouldn't have to do this just to get me in bed you know."

"Be serious. It's in my best interest to have you as part owner."

"Nice offer, look at the clunker and then ask me if I can afford to buy a piece of the pie."

"It will cost you nothing, and it isn't a gift either; you've earned it. Regardless of what you think, I have considered this before, but on the flight home I thought it through again. I'm at a point where I have to move on it. I don't want your money, Joanne. The only catch is that you have to hold on to your shares for five years before you can sell, giving me first option to buy you out. After that, you have the option to sell to me at market value, and if I don't want it you can go on the open market ... or keep building a nice investment. Sound good?"

"Uh ... yes but ..."

"Hell ... in five years from now I might want to retire or do something else. As a matter of fact ... you might eventually want to buy me out. Our agreement could give you first option before I sell. What do you believe would be a fair partnership?"

"Well, I don't want to sound greedy, but hey, you asked ... five percent would be nice."

"Uh, uh."

"Too greedy?"

"No, not at all, I want you married to this place and five percent won't do it but ten will. Give the two out front a raise and a bonus because we've had a damn good year so far. Go find yourself a company car and increase your salary by 20 %."

"I ... I don't know what to say. You look like you mean it, but it seems too good to be true. Things like this don't happen to me. What am I supposed to do now?"

"Say yes, get yourself a new four-wheel drive and call the lawyer to draw up the contract. Hey, we can afford it."

"What about the problems in Brazil, isn't that going to hurt us?"

"Yeah ... probably a little but we can easily make it up with the domestic lumber, besides, we have barely scratched the surface on the African Continent. I'm planning to go to the Ivory Coast later this year."

She threw her arms around me and accepted, after which she rushed out of the office just as Tracy and Denise came through the front door.

"What happened to Joanne?"

"Nothing … why?"

"She's crying."

"Probably, you women do the strangest things."

I closed the door when the phone rang. It was better to let Joanne give them the news about a raise. A week later I got a strange call.

"Mr. Swager, there is a call for you on line one."

"Hello?"

"Mr. Mickey Swager?"

"Yes."

"I'm Jack Ferranti, and I'm with the International Lumber Co. in Buffalo, New York. I understand that you import lumber direct from the loggers on the South American continent ."

"Yes, Mr. Ferranti. What can I do for you?"

"We have a little problem that we believe you can resolve for us."

"I'll try, but I don't have any stock. Any logs I import are already sold and shipped directly to my clients."

"I'm aware of that, but I understand you sometimes act as a broker."

"Yeah sometimes, but only under certain circumstances."

"Well, we are faced with something unusual. We have a

load of high-grade veneer logs in Honduras that needs to be shipped to Buffalo. I wonder if you could handle it for us."

"Why not have it transported yourself?"

"That's the problem. Our government has placed a temporary embargo on this commodity from that country, but there is a loophole. If we were to assign the shipment to you, you would own the goods which would allow us to purchase them from you, a Canadian source. Of course, you would have to go to Honduras to do the inspection and make all the arrangements as you normally do for yourself."

"That will add to your cost."

"I understand that. We have already purchased the merchandise on your behalf. All you need to invest is your time nothing more. Very attractive, don't you think, especially given your overall profit?"

"Look, Jack, I hope that you don't mind me calling you Jack?"

"By all means."

"What species is it?"

"Mahogany."

"Well, I don't want to be stuck with a load of mahogany if your broker can't clear it."

"No matter what, the risk is ours. Well gladly pay up front."

"I just came back from Brazil last week."

"I'm aware of that."

"You … how … who told you that? How did you know?"

"We inquired about you before making this offer, and I also happen to have a lady friend who is a flight attendant.

We went out last night, and your name popped up during dinner. You met her on your flight back."

"That's it, coincidence?"

"Uh ... yeah, you sound almost relieved ... or perhaps even disappointed. You weren't planning to ask her out yourself, were you?"

"Ha-ha, no ... although she was very attractive. I might be less apprehensive the next time I see her."

"So, we have a deal?"

"Sounds okay but why not send your own man?"

"That is what it is all about; we can't use an American to bring this commodity directly into the country. Are you interested?"

"Okay, courier me the documents and a Cashiers Check for $ 10,000, to cover expenses, and I'll make the arrangements. I can leave in two weeks."

I put the receiver down and thought about the wisdom of my decision. $10,000 for a few days work was well worth the risk. It would compensate for some of the losses in Brazil, and there could be a new supplier in it for me. Perhaps I should have investigated them more thoroughly, asked how they knew about me, or who had recommended me. It could be a trap to lure me out of the country, but it was too late now. I had to chance it. I couldn't very well run the business on the assumption that there might be a trap around every corner. Besides, someone determined enough to do me in, wouldn't be stopped by borders.

It was an unusual way of doing business, but I didn't always care about legalities, and in this particular deal, I had nothing to lose. Honduras didn't appeal to me because of its rebels and wars, but it was 13 degrees below zero in Montreal, and the climate in Honduras was a definite draw. I didn't want to leave until the deal with Joanne was signed and sealed. Two weeks later Joanne drove me to Dorval Airport in her new car.

7

The flight landed near La Ceiba on the northern coast of Honduras. Not expecting a welcoming party, I was surprised when an attractive young lady carried a sign with my name. She was tall, shapely, with curly black hair and a short-pleated skirt that complemented her beautiful slender legs. She came towards me before I even had a chance to present myself. She smiled and introduced herself as Berhinia Rojas, the daughter of Raimundo Rojas, who owned the mill where the logs I was to inspect, were stored. Her English was impeccable, the Spanish accent part of her charm. Her high heels made her about my height. Feeling a bit conspicuous in jeans and tee shirt, I wished that I had worn something less casual to make a better impression. Following her to the baggage area, I waited nervously expecting everything to be searched. I tried to look as if there was nothing to hide, but I had taken a small pistol apart and hidden the pieces in my shaving kit and other various items in my luggage. It had never been necessary before, but I was a wanted man now. With my bag on the counter, I started to open the zipper. Berhinia stepped forward, put her hand on top of it and leaned over whispering something in the agent's ear. He looked at her for a moment then smiled and nodded. She turned around and motioned a man standing nearby. He came over and closed the bag before carting it away towards the exit. I let out a sigh of relief.

"Is that all you brought?" she asked.

"Yes, I'll only be here for a couple of days."

"Moreno will put your bag in the car," she said as she slipped her arm through mine. I thought that she was rather forward but then, I didn't know what she had said to the customs agent. Moreno walked out the door, and I was about to follow, but Berhinia stopped me.

"We must wait, *Señor,*" she said in a hushed voice. "Moreno will let us know when it is safe."

"Safe ... from what?"

"Sssh, please *Señor* Swager, not so loud. *Banditos Señor,* we have many *banditos,* but you do not need to be concerned."

I looked uncomfortably around, failing to see her logic. How could I not be concerned with *banditos* close enough to make us whisper? Had I been a little too hasty accepting this assignment?

Moreno nodded after putting the luggage in the trunk. Berhinia let go of my arm and went out the door. Moreno held the car door open, and I saw the butt of a gun sticking out of his jacket. In addition to a chauffeur, he probably wore many more hats. Berhinia's skirt pulled up as she got into the car but she didn't bother adjusting it. I admired her while she stared innocently out the window. After a while, she moved closer and took my arm.

"So, Mr. Swager, what do you think of Honduras?" she asked with a smile.

"I'm sorry, but I don't know enough about your country. However, if we meet any *banditos*, I'll give you my opinion."

"Oh ... but, Mr. Swager," she laughed. "We have Moreno and the others to protect us. There is no reason to be nervous. Also, this car is ... bulletproof, yes?"

"Bulletproof ... okay, but what others?" I pointed to the glass partition, "I only see him."

"Oh no! Not just him, look out the back window."

I looked, and a couple of hundred feet behind was a Jeep with two men in it. I felt her staring at me. Our eyes met as I turned to face the front again and he saw how beautiful she was.

"I just love your blond hair, Mr. Swager. I have never been this close to a man with hair as blond yours. May I touch it?"

"Yes, you may and please ... call me Mickey or Mick. By the way, how do you spell your name?"

"B-e-r-h-i-n i-a. My mother is American-born, but she has always pronounced my name in Spanish, Berhinia but you may call me Virginia if you wish. I like it better."

She giggled as she ran her hand through my hair and crossed her legs. She squeezed my arm and sat as close as she could when she said, "my mother expects you to stay for the night. She has opened the beach house where you can sleep. My father snores very badly, and he would keep you awake."

"She shouldn't have bothered. I was planning to stay at a hotel in town."

"But, *Señor* ... I mean, Mickey, that would be too far away and too dangerous, and there are no nice places for you to stay in Zambuco. My father said that it would be better if you stayed with us. That way we can watch over you."

"Well ... if that's the way they feel I guess I'd better accept their hospitality."

"Oh that will be so good," she said as she squeezed my arm again.

Enjoying her none-too-subtle advances, I felt my chances for a pleasant time in Honduras were looking up.

Once out of the city, we drove west for about an hour with the ocean on the right and the wetlands to the left. Cinder block houses and shacks reminded me of the less fortunate in Brazil. I half listened to her chit-chat and couldn't help imagining what it would be like having a fling with her. Her none too subtle way of showing her interest was beginning to have an effect on what I considered my honorable intentions.

We drove through Zambuco and continued a few miles beyond the town and turned into a long driveway until we came to a gate. My guard was up. What if it were a trap set by the Senator? Moreno used the remote control to open it and continued past the buildings along a driveway that ended at a large, white stucco villa with a red clay-tile roof. It was magnificent, and the grounds were impeccable. The interlocking brick driveway didn't have a weed in it. It was a different world to the shacks we'd passed along the way. The car stopped in the courtyard, where a fountain spouted a stream of water as high as the villa and caused a clatter that almost drowned out the sound of the rolling surf. I could smell the ocean. The house backed right onto the beach.

Virginia walked me in. Heavy timbers outlined stucco panels on the ceiling. A wrought iron chandelier was suspended from a long chain, under which stood a fat little man whose white Panama hat matched his suit. The top of his hat wasn't any higher than my shoulder in spite of the fact that he wore elevated boots. He smiled hospitably. Virginia introduced him as Raimundo Rojas, her father. Looking rather comical with a big cigar in his left hand, he waddled towards us and extended his right hand. I would have preferred not to shake it, but I was intimidated enough to accept. When he noticed me looking at the holster under his arm, he shrugged, saying, "I'm sorry, *Señor* Swager ... *banditos,* you know, it is necessary, but there is no reason for you to worry about them. I have adequate men to protect you, but if you would like a gun, I can provide you with one."

"Oh no, *Señor,* I feel perfectly safe."

His English was adequate, but his accent made him difficult to understand. He was polite and pleasant yet; he made the hair on the back of my neck stand on end. I wasn't sure why but felt that I would have to be careful dealing with this little toad. Any man who carries a gun in his own home arouses suspicion. I didn't like him.

Rojas led me to his office. Unlike his good taste in architecture, his art collection didn't appeal to me. Rojas proudly showed his paintings and sculptures, explaining their artistic value and meaning. He pointed to a particularly ugly piece as his "Picasso." I much of the signature was smudged, almost illegible. Rojas explained that it was painted in his last years and the wine was to blame for his strange looking signature. It could have been Picasso. I took a closer look and saw, *"Pricasshole."*

My opinion of art is always sarcastic. In my view, art is, that it first be honest without needing the interpretation of a scholar who can turn a piece of crap into a valuable asset for a collector. If not, it is merely a financial investment or. I was politely listening to hear my host's interpretation of a statue displayed on a beautiful Brazilian rosewood pedestal. To me, the pedestal was more appealing than the statue and but waited to be enlightened.

"Oh, but *Señor* Swager ... this sculpture is my pride and joy. It represents the essence of a woman. You must have knowledge of art to see its beauty and artistic value."

I preferred looking at Rojas' daughter. Her essence looked quite different from what was standing on the pedestal, but I agreed politely.

"I'm sorry, *Señor,* my education has not been of a classical nature, I'm still learning to appreciate the finer things in life."

Rojas didn't answer but eyed me suspiciously.

The smell coming from the kitchen reminded me how hungry I was; it reminded me that I hadn't eaten since the airplane gourmet crap. Even the smoke of the *Señor's* cigar couldn't hide the aroma of the chef's work. Rojas asked me what my pleasure was, as he went over to the well-stocked bar. Tempted to say, Virginia, I decided not to stretch my luck. Looking surprised when I asked for a Southern Comfort, Rojas explained, "*Señor* ... I'm sorry, I do not have what you are requesting. I was informed that all Americans drink Scotch, no?"

"No, not all but it doesn't matter, *Señor,* Scotch with water will be fine."

"Oh, but please ... do call me Raimundo, yes?"

"Yes, *Señor,* if you will call me Mickey."

I didn't think that it was necessary to tell him that I was a Canadian as opposed to American. The business transaction didn't take long to complete, and by the time we were done, Raimundo was on his third glass of rum. He had probably been at the booze for a while, the way he slurred his words. His thumb was in the armhole of his vest; no longer trying to present a most appealing impression, he proudly displayed his fat belly and gun while holding a half-filled glass of booze in his other hand. Of course, his posturing was to let me know that he was important, someone to be reckoned with. Much to my relief, there was a knock on the door. Virginia came in to see if we were finished and ready for dinner. Rojas was beginning to talk more and more nonsense, and more Spanish words infiltrated his English. It didn't matter anymore whether I agreed or disagreed with what he said; he was too self-involved to care. With any luck, he would fall asleep during dinner and leave me alone with Virginia.

I declined his offer of another drink, but that didn't stop him from serving himself. He laughed loudly for some reason as he slapped my back to show camaraderie and reached up to rest his fat sausage hand on my shoulder. He kept it there while we followed Virginia to the dining room. He obviously needed my support to keep his balance. The sway of Virginia's hips and her long slender legs were interesting enough to distract me from "Rambling Raimundo," who was oblivious to me ogling his daughter. Virginia took no notice of him other than to pull out his chair and let him unceremoniously flop down. Virginia and I looked at each other. She shook her head and rolled her eyes as he continued his monolog in Spanish. I smiled politely; smiling at her came so easily. The table was set for four; maybe *Señora* Rojas would finally come on the scene.

Standing by the window, I admired the ocean. The sun cast a glimmering light across the waves. Virginia stood beside me and pointed to the horizon at islands that were part of Honduras. I didn't know why she did that; they were too far away to be seen. Perhaps it was an excuse to stand up close to me, and I enjoyed the moment. She acted as if we had known each other for a long time. Her hair brushed against my face while she spoke softly about her country. The smell of her perfume made me want to put my arm around her, but I maintained my business decorum. I didn't realize that someone else had entered the room until Raimundo stopped flapping his lips. Virginia was still firmly holding on to my arm, and I didn't object but fantasized having her with me in the beach house. She took my hand, "come Mickey, and sit with me," she suggested pointing to a chair, but I stood in shock staring at the lady who stood near the door. It must have been obvious because Virginia gave me a little tug, bringing me back to reality. Sometimes a woman ages with grace and poise that leaves a man breathless. This woman left me in that state. Her raven-black hair was shoulder length. She was as tall as Virginia but more beautiful. She gracefully walked towards me with a warm smile and extended hand.

"Mr. Swager, my name is Elizabeth Rojas. We are so pleased that you could join us. I hope that everything will be to your liking while you are here."

She spoke English without a distinguishable accent. She took her seat at the head of the table without waiting for my answer. Virginia must have caught my interest in her mother. Seated across from her, I sensed disappointment as Elizabeth led the conversation at the dinner table. I felt Virginia's stare. It was enough to make me uncomfortable. Finally, Elizabeth said, "forgive my daughter for staring at you, Mr. Swager, but we don't often have company. The city is too far away and the people of Zambuco ... well, you have seen how they live."

"I don't mind, ma'am, as a matter of fact, I am rather flattered. It isn't often that I'm blessed with the company of two beautiful ladies at the same table."

"You are most gracious, Mickey."

The difference between mother and daughter was also obvious in Elizabeth's general demeanor. In breeding, she far outclassed both Virginia and Raimundo. She was obviously well educated. Being a carpenter who had worked his way up to lumber merchant, I found her a bit intimidating at first, but her easy manner quickly put me at ease.

The food was delicious. The little toad never had a chance to taste it because he fell asleep before dinner could be served. Elizabeth gave the maid a sign; she left and returned with

Moreno. Together they helped Raimundo from his chair and out of the room as if it were an everyday occurrence. I probably was, he was a drunk, and neither Elizabeth nor Virginia made excuses for him. During the dinner conversation, Elizabeth often touched my hand as if it were a natural thing for her to do. It gave me an indescribably pleasant sensation. Each time she touched me, she left her hand a little longer. It must have irritated Virginia because she excused herself after finishing her coffee. Elizabeth and I stayed behind, and when she touched my hand again, she left it there. I took it and kissed it and watched her dark eyes scanning my face. I wanted to say things to impress her with my wit and intelligence, but the prospect of possible failure made my silence a better alternative.

We watched the crimson glow of the setting sun as we walked along the beach and listened to the sound of the rolling waves. She was less talkative. She put her arm around his my waist. I looked nervously back at the house. After a few more steps she stopped and looked at the setting sun. The tone of her voice dropped to reinforce how she felt. She sounded almost sad when she said, "how is it, Mickey, that love comes at the most inopportune times?"

I hesitated, we had met only two hours before, was it possible that she was referring to us? We had a romantic walk on the beach. Love had been on my mind, but her admission of her feelings gave me courage. Her sudden revelation left me little time for an appropriate response but the ball was in my court, and I was a natural seducer, or so I thought. I hoped that I would render her powerless before sundown.

"I don't know. Let's be grateful that we have this moment. I learned long ago that true love comes to everyone at least once, most of us only recognize it after it is too late."

It sounded good, and I was quite impressed with myself. I knew that there could be some of Victoria Tang's philosophy in that line, but time had made its origin doubtful, and that justified me claiming it as my own. She kept looking at me, almost smiling and she seemed moved by my corny statement.

"Will you love me tonight, Mickey? I know that it is wrong, but I want to be loved by a man I desire with all my heart. Once in my life, I want to be lustful and fulfilled. I want you, Mickey."

Never referring to our age difference, showing how secure she was broaching the subject. With tightness in my chest, I thought of how she could make me feel things that I had missed for over a decade. Her beauty, her body ... I didn't want just a moment with her; I wanted the whole night. Accepting her proposal too eagerly would make me seem desperate. I wanted to show her that I wasn't just any man. I didn't answer her and started to walk. She stepped in front of me. She looked at me pleadingly. She was close to tears. Holding her hands in mine, I pulled them behind her back and felt her breasts pressing against me as I kissed her and she pressed her knee between my legs.

"Oh, please love me tonight Mickey. God is forgiving, he will grant me this moment of indiscretion. I have never known a man like you and I may never again."

God wasn't on my mind. I didn't believe that making love

was a sin, although her adultery probably was. I kissed her tenderly and led her to the beach house. Seeing my luggage, she smiled and said, "I was hoping that you would stay the night, but I didn't think it would be with me."

I silently pulled her down on the bed. The experience with her boosted my already inflated ego. Inexplicably the sex I experienced was out of this world. We stayed in bed, and we watched it spread the beauty of the sunrise, glorifying the Caribbean. Elizabeth got up. We kissed for the last time before we walked back to the main house. She held my hand, and she didn't seem to care if anyone saw us.

After breakfast and back alone in the beach house, I meticulously assembled my gun. After a thorough inspection of its functionality, I strapped it to my leg and left. Although I was sad leaving, it was better to go as soon as possible. Pursuing a relationship with her was totally unrealistic.

It was close to ten in the morning by the time Raimundo came to the yard. I had already started the inspection and the tally of the logs. Oddly enough, the logs were kept inside one of the warehouses. Veneer logs were usually stored outside and kept wet to prevent cracking.These logs were of the highest quality with a high moisture content. The tally, however, showed a shortage on every log. Rojas followed me around like a puppy. His foreman checked one of the logs and agreed with me that there was a discrepancy. I looked at the nearby guard who carried an assault rifle. Rojas shrugged and said, "the financial cost of replacing the logs is excessively greater than the extra security required to keep them from being stolen. Thieves, Mr. Swager, *banditos,* we never know here, this is not like America."

He belched unceremoniously, without an apology and adjusted the documentation without objection. I was used to loggers disputing my way of tallying, and I couldn't understand why he didn't. It struck me that he wasn't as friendly as he had been the night before. Perhaps he was hungover. I shook hands with the little toad and got into the limo ... alone.

The limo left the yard ahead of the trucks, and by the time Moreno turned the corner onto the main road, they were already out of sight.

The drive along the highway was most pleasant. Strangely, I saw no evidence of any other logging traffic. I began to wonder. Why was Rojas' business so far from others in the logging industry? He had no manufacturing facilities. This was evidenced by the fact that I had not heard any of the usual sounds of machinery. Besides, the few logs he had wouldn't have been enough to keep him in business nor support his lavish lifestyle. I would have to take another look at these logs. Perhaps there was more to this deal than I had been led to believe. I began to feel uneasy ... something wasn't quite right here. After all, this was Latin America; drugs could be involved. I took a deep breath and realized that it would be too dangerous to show any suspicions. I was glad when the city came into view. At least after the logs were safely in the hold of the ship, I could expect the armed escort to vanish. Taking my pistol, I checked it once more before replacing it in the holster. If it came down to a fight, I might be forced to use it. If Moreno even knew I had a gun, he didn't seem to care. It was dangerous to have it on me, but the longer I was in the country, the more justified I felt carrying it. I'd never felt this uneasy anywhere else. Moreno let me off at a small dilapidated hotel near the loading docks. La Ceiba had the convenience of both an airport and a harbor. The *El Tigro* had seen better days. There was more rust than paint on her hull. The captain generously offered me the opportunity to sail along with the cargo, but I declined. The trucks arrived fifteen minutes later, and loading began immediately. My suspicions grew when Moreno chewed out the crane operator for almost dropping a log. Sauntering over to one of the waiting trucks, I took another look. A guard followed me closely. The logs had been recently cut on both ends and judging by the logging marks; they were not made in the forest. If the logs had been tampered with, a good job of had been done covering it up. There were some minor details, however, that only an expert would see. This evidence I saw accounted for and the shortage of the tally. The tally had obviously been made by the logger who sold the logs, not by Rojas or his men after they had been tampered with. I didn't want the ever-present guard to know of my suspicions and assuming he understood English asked him for a knife. Without hesitation, he reached over his shoulder and pulled a dagger out of the scabbard on his back. I used it to pry a tiny piece of fungus from a crevice of a log and gave the knife back. I examined it intently. Showing it to the guard, I explained about the Canadian laws on importing contaminated materials and vegetation. He took one more look at the piece in my hand, shrugged and walked away. He'd understood though, because he walked along the side of the truck and picked a piece from another log, looked back and appeared to be satisfied that I hadn't discovered anything. He walked away smiling. Glad to be dismissed so easily, I was now even more convinced that I had been drawn into a drug-smuggling operation. The only way to confirm it was to trace the shipment to its final destination. My client was in a well-known, legitimate business but perhaps there was someone on the inside using me as a mule. It would be dangerous but necessary to find out what was really going on. I had to go through with the deal, or I could very well be developing another deadly enemy. The loading was completed by late afternoon with the ship scheduled to sail the next morning. After more than 12 years of traveling the world, I had found that the smell of bunker oil was the universal odor of the world's ports; La Ceiba was no different. Taking a stroll along the shore, I was intrigued by the sounds from a nearby cantina. I went inside. Not surprisingly, I didn't exactly blend in. My blond hair was a curiosity. I walked over to the bar, and I was suddenly aware of what it was like to be a minority. I ordered a beer planning to take it to a vacant table in a far corner of the room. The stench of booze and cigarillo smoke was overwhelming. I should never have gone in, but I was thirsty and besides, it would give me an opportunity to observe the local people. There were times when prospective clients asked about the various places where I transacted business, and it was good to be able to give some insight, even if it were gained in a common bar Someone tripped me, and I spilled my beer over the floor. I recovered without falling and apologized to the man who still had his boot way out in the aisle. The man as short as Rojas, but skin over bone, stood up. Obviously, the apology wasn't enough. He turned his head sideways and said something in Spanish that must have been amusing because the other patrons laughed. The way he looked around the room for approval reminded me of Silver King. Not interested in getting into a fight, I turned to leave but looked back when the crowd roared. The "bandito" waved a knife; it needed no interpretation. He wanted to teach the gringo a lesson while providing entertainment. The cantina became quiet. All eyes were fixed on the two of us. Without the knife, it would have been no contest, but the knife and the audience made a huge difference. To run would be too dangerous. I stepped back, raising my hands to show that I wasn't armed. My attacker could have reconsidered and saved face, but he wanted blood. He lunged forward in an effort to stab me, but I jumped back. Switching the knife from hand to hand, he kept slashing in my direction. His enjoyment of the game was accelerated by the encouragement of the crowd. I saw how fired-up he was. His yellow teeth separated his skinny lips into thin lines. Sweat was running down his face, and his wide grin confirmed his pleasure. The gun, strapped to my leg, was useless. To bend down and pull it from the holster would give my opponent ample time to stab me. It wouldn't have bothered me to shoot him but to do so in front of so many witnesses was dangerous. With each slash, his friends egged him on, *ole*! They wanted blood. I had made a major tactical error when I initially started to back away; I had not headed for the door. People who had been standing behind me since the first slash had moved aside to make room. I heard the tables and chairs being dragged across the floor. The knife came closer. I was cornered. The last slash nicked my shirt. I bent over to reach for my gun expecting to be stabbed, but nothing happened. Why had he stopped? He couldn't have known that I was armed. Stranger still, he wasn't even looking at me. He stared intently over my shoulder. I was afraid to move, so I stood still. Moreno's voice came from behind me, and I glanced back. His gun was aimed at the bandito as he spoke. At the mention of the name Rojas my assailant quietly went back to his table and sat down. Relieved, I turned to thank Moreno, but he was gone.

I left the cantina the way I had come, thirsty but I had no stomach to go anywhere else for a beer. My adventurous spirit was gone, and I returned to the relative safety of my hotel. The Rojas name obviously carried clout. Looking out the window, I saw Moreno patiently leaning against a streetlight, smoking, seeming to ignore me. The ocean breeze carried the smoke of his cigarillo through the open window. Somehow, the smell was comforting, and I slept. My last thought before dozing off was how inhospitable the country was, with the exception of Elizabeth, of course.

8

A full moon provided enough light for me to assess my surroundings. I stood in an alley, in the shadow of a warehouse. I knew the docks weren't safe. Even the police avoided patrolling there after dark. I was unarmed and on hostile turf but I had to find out if my suspicions were justified. The ship could have unloaded her cargo at any port along the way and, but that was not the case. She had entered the St. Lawrence Seaway at Montreal, confirming her destination was as planned. If she anchored out on the lake, it would be safe to spend the night in my hotel room, if not, the night would be long, cold and sleepless.

A chilling breeze blew in from the lake. Not dressed for the cool evening I pulled the collar of my jacket up, cursing myself for being so naïve on this scale "getting involved in a drug-running operation into the US could put me in jail for a very long time" I mumbled. Suddenly something hard poked my back, and a man's voice quietly told me not to make any noise or sudden moves.

"Hey, don't be embarrassed," he added. "We all talk to ourselves once in a while but another peep out of you, or a stupid move, will shut your fucking yap forever, so don't fuck with me ... got that?"

"Yeah, I got that."

I wasn't anxious to call his bluff when he shoved me up against the wall. The gun remained in my back while I was frisked. To my surprise, My wallet went untouched. I feverously contemplated my options as I was led down the alley to where a long black limousine stood, its engine softly purring. It hadn't been there when I arrived and certainly was not the typical car driven by an average thug. The rear passenger door was wide open, but I couldn't see inside. An Edward G. Robinson type with a cigar in his mouth, pointing a gun at me, would have fit the occasion. But ...

"Good evening, Mr. Swager, welcome to Buffalo. Please join me."

I was somewhat relieved to hear a woman's voice because I never associated the same degree of violence with women as men.

She sounded pleasant enough, but I wasn't eager to accept her invitation. Her flashlight blinded me when I answered, "no thanks I like it better out here."

I heard her chuckle as the gun jabbed my spine again. The gunman pushed me into the seat opposite her. He put his gun back in its holster, and he stood next to the open door. I couldn't see much of her but sensed her stare. She turned the light off. When my eyes adjusted to the dark, I began to make out her form. She was looking me over from head to toe, and I felt about as uncomfortable as I had with the gun in my back moments before. She sounded sincere when she said how unfortunate it was that we were meeting under such circumstances.

"You're better looking than your pictures, Mr. Swager, or may I call you Mickey?"

"Since I am your prisoner, ma'am, you can call me just about anything you like."

"Call me Amelia; I'm Amelia Galante. Consider yourself my guest; prisoner sounds so unfriendly. You'll see that I am not *all* bad, once you get to know me."

"Forgive me. I prefer not to know you at all. Here," I said, taking the wallet out of my pocket. "Take it; there isn't much in it. You should pick a better class neighborhood to conduct your business."

"Oh dear," she laughed. "I don't want your wallet."

"Then what do you want? My body isn't as young as it used to be and the smell after a hard day's work makes it even less attractive?"

"I'll get over it."

"Lady, based on what I see, it is hard to imagine that you are so desperate for a man's company that you have to resort to kidnapping. Take my word for it; most men would give anything for the pleasure of your company."

"Does that include you, Mr. Swager?"

"Hardly, I have better things to do than cater to the whims of a spoiled brat. All I want is to get home and hit the shower. Get your kicks elsewhere."

Abruptly, she ordered the man outside to take them

home. He was about to get in the back with us when she snapped, "no Louie ride up front with Robbie."

"Okay, but I'll cuff him first," he said as he grabbed my jacket yanking me out of the car before she had a chance to say anything. I stumbled and fell up against Louie who almost lost his balance. He tried to steady us both which gave me a chance to get his gun. He grabbed my wrist as we struggled, but I managed to twist it and point it at Louie's chest. I saw the terror in his eyes when I managed to pull the trigger, and he sagged slowly to the ground. I was about to run but I'd momentarily forgotten about Robbie.

"You're gonna have to turn around to shoot me. I already got my piece aimed right at your fucking ass! You better drop it, I get pissed-off when I'm kept waiting."

I turned around and faced a huge black man who towered over me. He was holding a howitzer aimed at my belly. I dropped the gun and raised my hands. Robbie grinned and shoved me against the limo. He picked up the gun and stuck it in his belt. He checked on Louie while keeping his eyes on me.

"He's dead, ma'am, Louie's dead ... the son-of-a-bitch killed him."

Leaning forward she looked at the body and snarled, "damn! How could he be so stupid!"

"You want me to have this piece-a-shit put him in the trunk, ma'am?"

"No, Robbie, leave him ... he's dead anyway. I'll call Dad to send a couple of guys to pick him up. Get Swager in the car and get us the hell out of here. That shot was loud enough to wake up the whole damn city."

Still hoping to come out in one piece I said, "I am very sorry, I didn't mean to shoot; I just wanted to get away from him. It just went off; it was an accident."

She didn't answer. Neither she nor Robbie seemed to broken-up over Louie's death. They were more concerned about the sound of the shot. Amelia fell back in her seat. Robbie pulled the handcuffs out of Louie's pocket and cuffed my hands behind my back. When he opened the door to put me next to him in the passenger seat, Amelia called out, "It's okay Robbie, he"ll ride with me."

Amelia reached into her purse and pulled out a gun. Its nickel finish flashed in the moonlight when she pointed it at me. She slid across the seat making room for me to get in. Without concern for my comfort, Robbie pushed my head down and shoved me into the car. I fell to the floor between the seats; my feet were hanging out of the limo. Robbie showed no pity, kicking them repeatedly.

"Giddup you sucker!" he said. "Giddup you son-of-a-bitch!"

After watching me struggling to obey him, he grabbed the handcuffs and yanked me up. It felt as if my arms were being twisted from their sockets, but I finally managed to seat myself next to the lovely Amelia.

"No, not here ... there!" she snapped, pointing her gun to the opposite seat.

Robbie started the limo, and Amelia picked up the phone and called daddy. After telling him what had happened on the dock, and that they were on their way, she turned her attention back to her "guest." She stared at me for a moment and then said with a soft and pleasant voice, "I'm sorry for all this, Mickey … I didn't plan for any rough stuff. You know, things could have been so much nicer, if the circumstances had been different."

There was nothing nice about being kidnapped or having Robbie kick the hell out of me. I didn't want to antagonize her, but couldn't resist letting her know how I felt and answered sarcastically, "Oh, don't be so apologetic. It could have been a lot worse. I could be the one lying dead in that alley. I don't know what you're up to, but I don't consider meeting you under any circumstance pleasant. You're responsible; you came looking for this, remember."

She showed no remorse over the loss of her bodyguard, nor did she acknowledge my sarcasm.

"What do you want from me?" I asked.

"My father wants to ask you a few questions."

"Oh … okay … I feel a lot better now. You had me worried for a moment … When daddy is finished with me, you'll let me walk away of course. You'll let me walk right into the first police station I can find … right?"

"I doubt that you will, Mickey, I doubt that very much."

"That's what I figured. When daddy's done with me, I'll be taken for a ride, and my carcass will be dumped in a sewer somewhere."

"Don't be so morbid. You won't be killed. As a matter of fact, you won't even be hurt if you don't do anything more stupid things."

The conversation ended, and we drove on, staring at each other. I tried to figure out what she wanted and who she was. This obviously had something to do with the logs in the El Tigro's cargo hold. Why was she sent to kidnap me? I understood Mafia women were kept out of the business affairs. She was beautiful. It struck me that there was something very familiar about her ... I just couldn't figure out what it was.

She put the gun back in her purse and stared out the window. Flawless from every angle she reminded me a little of Elizabeth. My thoughts went back to Honduras and the night at the beach house. Was this my life flashing by, before being executed? Someone as beautiful as Amelia had to have some tenderness. She didn't look like a killer, but she had shown a tougher side when she just left Louie dead in the alley and pointed her gun at me.

The limo finally stopped in front of heavy iron gates. A man, with a rifle slung by a strap over his shoulder, came out from the shadow and peered into the driver's window. He opened the gates, and we drove through, and I felt trapped as the gates closed. The car stopped, and Robbie got out. He opened the door for Amelia. I followed. The sound of barking dogs intensified my ominous feeling of danger. We stood under a large portico that extended over the front door of a huge brick house with large leaded glass windows. The entrance door was decorated with heavy black iron hardware. Floodlights were everywhere. A couple of bored armed men gawked at us. The rooster on the cupola of the carriage house stood silhouetted against the clear evening sky and squeaked as it moved in the breeze. I took a deep breath hoping it wouldn't be my last. Amelia waited at the top step, taking no notice of the man with the shotgun standing beside her; she seemed perfectly at ease in such a hostile environment.

"Come on," she said, "let's go in, daddy is waiting."

Not anxious to meet daddy, a shove in my back from Robbie reminded me who was in charge and I followed her. The inside of the mansion was as impressive as outside. Wood paneling covered the entrance hall walls, and a huge crystal chandelier hung from an elaborately decorated ceiling. Thick rugs muffled our steps. I moved on after another "gentle" prompt. Amelia stopped at a door, knocked softly and entered the room. She left the door open, and with yet another shove from Robbie, I was almost knocked to the floor. This appeared to annoy her.

"Knock it off!" she snapped. "There's no need for that crap!"

Robbie didn't answer and followed us into the room. The walls were lined from floor to ceiling with books. A ladder with rollers attached to a railing ran along the top of the shelves. I had only ever seen such a contraption in movies. Heavy, dark-red velvet drapes covered the windows. Four large wingback chairs stood in pairs, in front of a huge fireplace where a Great Dane rested comfortably. He raised his head for a moment, sighed, and let it rest on the foot of a small, frail, old man sitting in one of the chairs. His hair was snow-white, and his face was as wrinkled as a dried apple. A big man stood statue-like beside the fireplace. He left only when the old man pointed at him and waved his hand without even looking at him. Amelia leaned over and kissed the little man's cheek, and the dog wagged his tail. Her voice and scent were familiar to him, but its eyes were fixed on me. The room was dimly lit allowing the flickering fire to reflect on the old man's face. Ignoring his daughter, he continued to stare into the fire as he gently swirled a partly filled brandy snifter. She didn't seem surprised at his attitude.

"Daddy, Mr. Swager is here."

He didn't answer but took a sip of his brandy and kept staring at the fire. A small column of smoke rose from a cigar in his other hand. The whole scene looked and felt as if it came straight out of an old gangster movie. The dog sighed and moved his head from the man's foot to the rug. The white fur around his nose testified to his old age. It was clear that he and his master had been together for many years. He didn't sleep because a stranger was near. I knew enough about dogs not to be misled by his apparent tolerance of me. The old man cleared his throat. He spoke in a gravelly, raspy voice, probably cultivated by years of smoking his cigars and drinking his brandy. Without looking at me, he said, "you can understand, Mr. Swager, that I am not pleased about the loss of a good and loyal man. He had been with me for many years."

He spoke slowly with each word carefully chosen. He paused, and I took it as the cue for my answer.

"I apologize for the unfortunate incident, sir but it wasn't my intention to shoot him. Besides, he was obviously not good enough to be in your service. His carelessness could have cost you your daughter's life."

My words, I thought, were equally well chosen but I held my breath. Using the word "obviously" wasn't smart. It could have been taken as a criticism of his ability to know his employees. I didn't have a clue about how to speak to a gangster, let alone one who seemed to enjoy such a high rank! I would have to watch what I said in future.

When I spoke, the dog had raised its head and changed his position, resting his head on his front paws. He kept switching his eyes between his master and me as if he were trying to see who would speak next. I hadn't moved since entering the room and waited for a reaction to what I'd said. The old man looked at me for the first time and slowly took another puff from his cigar. His cold blue eyes looked deadly through the cloud of smoke and sent a shiver down my spine.

"I know, I know ... perhaps you're right, maybe he was getting too sloppy," he said with disgust. "Sit down Swager, sit ... sit, don't stand there ... you make me uncomfortable."

"Sir, I can't ... I mean, these handcuffs ... if you would ..."

He didn't give me a chance to finish.

"Take off the cuffs, Robbie, and leave us ... he's harmless, besides Amelia is here."

He must have been sure that Amelia wouldn't hesitate to shoot if necessary. Robbie removed the handcuffs and left the room.

"Sit down, Swager. My daughter will make you a drink. What would you like?"

I was tempted to say, freedom, but said, "I'll have a Southern Comfort ... if you have any, that is."

It would probably help to ease my tense disposition.

I watched Amelia cross the floor to the bar. She was

lovely. I was still intrigued by the thought of knowing her from somewhere. It was most distracting.

"We were expecting you, Mr. Swager," she smiled as she handed me my favorite drink. I was surprised that daddy kept Southern Comfort in his bar. I was confused. I had come in expecting to be shot, and here I was being treated like a guest. Contentedly puffing on his cigar, daddy obviously didn't care about my unwillingness to be there.

"You need not look so puzzled, Swager, my daughter, was very thorough when she investigated you. I was kept informed about your activities as you followed the ship through the St. Lawrence Seaway. My daughter even predicted that you would be in the harbor. Having you brought here was easy because you are so predictable."

He continued without missing a beat.

"By the way, what did you expect to find, snooping around the docks? There is nothing to see. Everything closes down at night."

"You probably know already, sir, I have a shipment of logs on board the El Tigro, and I have to see that it gets here intact."

"Why pay so much attention to this shipment. If you work with the right shipping company, there shouldn't be any reason for concern, should there? The recipient of the merchandise would certainly contact you if there were a problem, wouldn't he?"

"Well ... yes, sir, but actually, I am the shipping company. I'm responsible as long as I have title to the cargo."

He suddenly turned, stared angrily at me and shouted,

"let's cut the crap, shall we! We both know that you are bullshitting."

"I sure as hell don't want them to fall into the wrong hands. I love life too much to lose it over some drug-smuggling scheme. And for the record, I suspect that the shipment is probably yours and if it is, let me tell you that I resent the fact that you have used my good name and my firm in your dirty business."

The old man calmed down.

"You speak boldly young man … very boldly."

"You told me to cut the crap, and that's exactly what I am doing."

Daddy continued puffing on his cigar. His glass was empty, and Amelia went to refill it as if it were her duty. She hadn't interfered in the discussion. She sat quietly in her chair, looking at me. Her eyes smiled, possibly even flirted. It seemed this meeting with daddy wasn't strictly business, at least not as far as she was concerned. As the daughter of a mobster, she made me damn uncomfortable.

Daddy brought me back to reality.

"Since I now know you have those suspicions, what makes you think that I'll let you leave?"

"Because killing me would eventually reveal my whole involvement in this affair. I'm not as naïve as you think. I had taken some precautions before I came to Buffalo."

He stared coldly at me and barked furiously, "you dare to blackmail me, you try to scare me … me, Alphonse Galante?"

His face was beet red.

"No. I want nothing from you except to be left alone.

Tomorrow or the next day, that shipment will clear customs and me, may God forgive me, will legally be as involved as you. Pleading innocence in front of a judge would be useless, we both know that. But, we both also know that if you choose to get rid of me, all hell will break loose. The document is in a very secure place and will only be destroyed once I know that I'm safe."

"First of all, don't bring God into this, Swager. He created the raw materials and the intellect of man to make the product. Those facts make begging for his absolution unnecessary. Secondly, I find you a very distrusting individual."

"Well yeah ... you can hardly blame me for looking out for myself."

"Your ignorance about my way of doing business is misleading you, Swager; violence is a thing of the past. We're not monsters, regardless of your perception of us. Besides, don't flatter yourself, you're not that important for us to take that kind of risk."

He had an arrogant little smirk.

"By the way, how did you find out about the contents of the shipment? Where did we go wrong?"

"You made the mistake of hiring me; I'm an expert. Lumber is my business. There were several things that made me suspect someone had tampered with the logs. If I were to reveal what I believe, I could be considered a willing participant in any future shipments."

"I hired you on the recommendation of Rojas. He was insistent that you handle things. I was apprehensive when he approached me with the deal because he is not the sharpest knife in the butcher block, but he said that he could guarantee the merchandise would arrive intact ... I gather he was right on the mark. Apparently, you have a good reputation in the lumber business."

"Yeah ... as it turns out, your perfect patsy, I sure as hell hope that the customs agents don't have a dog sniffing around. If the authorities get wind of this, I'll be finished as an importer, and I'll probably land in jail."

"You don't have to worry about that, Swager. The shipment has already been through several dog-sniffing tests and came up negative. Rojas knows that he won't see a cent if the goods are lost. That's exactly why you had title to the merchandise. If things were to go wrong, you would be the one left holding the bag. I'll give you a break, you can sign the documents over to me now, and I'll have the shipment cleared by my broker."

I was relieved! The old man watched me as I signed the papers and handed them over to him.

"The balance of the payment for your service will be sent to your office. There is no need to send an invoice. The less paper, the better."

"Then what was all this cloak and dagger stuff with Jack Ferranti."

"We had to get you for the job somehow. You would never have transported the merchandise willingly if you had known what was in it. You realize, of course, that I could make you talk and you wouldn't be able to hide behind any evidence."

"You just told me a moment ago, that you weren't

monsters and now you talk about torturing me; a hell of a contradiction isn't it? Yeah … you can make me talk, but by now you must realize that I am as driven by my convictions as you are by yours. You know that I can't talk about this to anyone; I would be cutting my own throat. Perhaps in time, we can forget we have ever met."

He turned away. Amelia sat quietly beside her daddy, innocently looking at me, yet all the while the gun in her purse proved how she lived. The old man didn't look at me, but he spoke again as if thinking aloud.

"I could use a man like you. I would pay you well … but then, I guess that your damn principles would get in the way. You know something? During prohibition, everyone who sold booze was a criminal. Today the people who sell booze are respectable businessmen. Alcohol is no less a drug than heroin or cocaine. Perhaps in time people will come to accept this fact. Authorities call me a criminal, but they create the opportunity to make a profit, for them as well as for me. Imagine the loss to the economy of this country. Drugs are big business for the government. They wouldn't be able to deal with all the unemployed policemen and agents spread around the world. The government is the biggest launderer of drug money. All the money seized goes right back into circulation. America's jails would be half-empty if drugs were legal. The DEA would be history, and their agents would have to look for other opportunities to line their pockets. No, my friend, I'm not a criminal. I'm only someone who sees the chance to make a buck … anyway …" his voice trailed off, "my daughter will see that you get back to your hotel. I don't think that I have to worry about you. Amelia was right with her report, and you're too practical and smart to be a danger to me. As a matter of fact, I kind of like you."

He waved his hand in the very same way he had when he had dismissed his bodyguard earlier, and he didn't bother to say good-bye. Amelia got up and took my arm. She didn't seem to care that her father was still in the room. She looked into my eyes as if she were trying to say something.

The dog stood up and slowly walked over to us and sniffed my feet.

"Nice dog, what's his name?"

"Sammy One Wag."

"One Wag?"

"Yes, it used to be Samson. But he usually wags his tail only once. My brother, Mario, says that he doesn't want to wear out his butt and he's lazy. He's harmless."

"I never consider any dog harmless."

Samson sniffed a few more times and returned to his master. He would remember me the next time. Amelia kissed daddy on the cheek, started for the door, I followed her.

I expected to be sent back by cab, but Amelia led me to the limo and got in ahead of me. If it were going to be another typical Mafia ride, she was cool about it. Her purse, with her gun, was on the seat across from me. I didn't know if I'd fooled her and the old man with my bluff, but it looked like I had pulled it off and my business with him was finished.

She linked arms with me as if we were friends. Her hands were soft and small but as I'd already witnessed, large enough to hold a gun. The glass partition behind the driver was closed, and we were alone when she said, "do you believe in love at first sight, Mickey?"

She caught me by surprise. What-the-hell was she up to? She looked straight at me and continued, "I think that it is happening to me. I think I'm falling in love with you."

She bowled me over.

"Yeah ... right, and I suppose the gun in your purse is a cigarette lighter? You kidnapped me for Christ sake! What are you going to do next? Kiss me or blow my brains out? I don't know nor do I want to. You must be nuts coming out with crap like that."

She reached for her purse, took out the gun and popped the clip.

"See, real bullets!" she snapped putting it back in the gun, slamming it expertly in place in the palm of her hand. She tossed it in my lap and slid back in the seat saying, "keep it if you like."

Perhaps I wasn't going to be fish-food after all. I gave the gun back, and she put it in her purse. She must have suspected my interest in her. Interest? Hell! I was fascinated! But it was only her body that was the attraction. She became bolder as we neared the hotel. She tapped on the window behind the driver, and he opened it.

"Pull over at the next gas station and have a smoke, Robbie."

He didn't answer but closed the window and pulled over a block further and got out of the limo.

"I have known about you for quite some time, Mickey. You are no stranger to me. I became interested in you after

I started my investigation. I studied your pictures and read everything I could find out about you. I may be new to you, but I probably fell in love with you a long time ago but didn't realize it until I met you. I get a strangely pleasant feeling just touching you. I can't help it, it's true. I know that I'm just a kid to you but what difference does that make? You must have had similar feelings some time or other.

"Look, Amelia, it doesn't matter what I feel or what has happened to me. I don't even know you ... shit ... I don't want to know you! If things were different ... well ... sure ... you are very attractive. But everything you have done has put my life and my business in jeopardy. Abducted at gunpoint, almost killed by one of your goons, you have involved me in a drug-running operation, and you sit here talking as if I should feel lucky that you are infatuated with me. Can't you see that you are totally illogical? When I think of that gun in your purse, I see death waiting to happen."

"There is no logic to love! I know what I've done is wrong in your eyes but I wasn't born to a normal family. I only have my father and brother as examples. My mother died giving birth to me. I know what you are going to say, "that's no excuse," and I know it isn't. Meeting you is giving me a much broader look at life ... I can change ... I know I can."

"After investigating me, you should realize how different I am from you. I hope to have a normal relationship someday, maybe even get married and raise a family. You don't fit into that picture."

"You don't even have anyone in mind. I on the other hand already know who I want to marry. It may take some doing, but I'll fight like hell to get you. I know that I'm running ahead of myself, but you're leaving tomorrow ... there's just no time ... and I can't help how I feel."

The sincerity in her beautiful eyes, her lovely face, her gentle touching, and the smell of her perfume, played havoc with my senses. I simply had to get out of this situation. I believed myself to be a master at the game of seduction, but she was better. I had to let her know that I wasn't prepared to be killed over a one night stand.

"I'm sorry ... but you're barking up the wrong tree."

"Would you give up if you were in love with someone?"

"If the situation were as impossible as this one ... yeah, I would. As a matter of fact, what you feel is probably not love at all but a teenage crush. Now, will you please take me back to my hotel, better yet, call me a cab. This situation is impossible for us both and I have no intention of continuing this insanity."

She didn't say anything more and called Robbie. She held onto my arm firmly. I didn't stop her when she rested her head against my shoulder. Too soon, the limo stopped at the hotel, and she reluctantly let go of my arm. I saw her eyes getting moist. It wasn't easy walking across the parking lot knowing that her eyes were following me. I weakened ... and winced when I saw the reflection of the limo lights in the hotel doors. An affair with her would not have been a one night stand, but it could have lasted a lifetime, however long or short it would be in my case. The limo was still parked at the far end of the driveway. I just couldn't turn and look because I didn't want her to think I changed my mind.

A bellhop came towards me as soon as I entered and he gave me a note. I read it as I walked towards the elevator.

"Please Mr. Swager, meet me outside as soon as you get this note, very urgent!"

I didn't know anyone in the area, and supposedly, no one knew where he was. How did the bellhop know me? I hesitated. Perhaps it was Amelia ... but that wasn't possible she had been with me ever since we first met on the dock. Besides, she had had her say. Had her father arranged something ahead of time? Intrigued and puzzled I walked back out and noticed that the limo hadn't moved. I looked around. There didn't seem to be anyone approaching or waiting. Suddenly a gunshot echoed. There was a strange sensation in my chest, then a burning pain. I slowly sagged down realizing I'd been shot. I saw a small tear in my shirt and a patch of bright, red blood. The shooter was a pro, aiming for my heart. Amelia came running towards me. She knelt down and tried to hold me upright, but I sagged sideways on her lap. With my head cradled in her arms, I knew I was dying. Was she so twisted or obsessed with me that she had me shot? I'd often prayed for death during the lonely nights after I lost Maggie. I couldn't help but smile. My life was ending under a clear sky, in a hotel parking lot. I looked up at the sky and saw the stars. As a child, I had been taught that the soul goes to heaven after death. But I didn't believe in heaven I focused on the brightest star, hoping it to be mine.

The pain was gone, I was numb and short of breath. I had always believed death to be as natural as birth. I now experienced that it was just as I imagined, soft and gentle, not vengeful but forgiving. I was paying my dues for the mistakes of my life. I'd lived by the sword, so I felt no need to forgive her. I felt at peace in the arms of my assassin while her tears dripped onto my face as she frantically screamed for help.

9

Oxygen hissed, and monitors beeped. A nurse lifted my head to let me drink through a straw. I remembered Amelia holding me after I had been shot, nothing more. The nurse put my head back on the pillow, and I fell asleep. Sometime later, I saw a man in a white coat talking to a nurse. He was about to leave when someone else came in.

"Is he ready to talk, Doc?"

"I don't think that it is a good idea, it's too soon, only the immediate family for now."

"How bad is he?"

"Well, he was damn lucky, the projectile bounced off a rib and was lodged between the aorta and pulmonary artery near the upper part of his heart, a fraction off either way, and he'd be dead."

"Look, Doc, the longer we wait, the harder it's going to be to find the shooter. Besides, he doesn't have any family here."

Well ... okay, but make it short, we repaired the damage, but he's lost a lot of blood."

The doctor left, stuffing his stethoscope into his pocket.

"Mr. Swager, I'm detective Philip Litvack, and this is my partner Sam Doman. We would like to ask you some questions about the night you were shot."

I stared at him for a moment. The fog began to lift. Slowly, it all came back. There was some pain in my chest. Otherwise, I felt okay. I also realized that I had to be careful and not say anything that could get me into more trouble with the Galante family. The best way to gain some time, before giving these cops any answers was to act as if I were in bad shape or was suffering from a memory lapse. The nurse stayed and took my pulse. There was a tap on the window, and she looked up to see who was at the door.

"That girl has been waiting all night," she said, "I thought that she'd gone, but she must have come back. It looks like she changed her clothes, she was covered in blood."

"Who is it?" I asked

"I don't know she came with you in the ambulance. Look," she said raising my head. The detectives waited patiently. It was Amelia. The fact that she was there could only mean that she wasn't involved. No matter how dangerous she or her family were, it was better to be under their protection, than to be thrown in jail for drug running.

"Okay, let her in."

"No!" said detective Doman, "she has to wait until we are finished."

"Hey! Either she comes in, or you are finished right now."

He pointed his finger at me as if to make sure that I understood how serious he was.

"You're interfering with an official police investigation."

"Go to hell. I don't give a damn about your official investigation. I'm the one who got shot, remember? I'm not the criminal, or perp, to use your term. This is my room if you don't like it, leave!"

Doman continued: "the doctor has restricted visitors to family only."

"Then what the hell are you doing in here? She's my lawyer for Christ sake! I'm not going to answer any more questions until you let her in here. Better yet ... get the hell out of here!"

"Now why would you need a lawyer if you haven't done anything wrong, just tell me that?"

"Hey, I'm what you guys call a foreign national. I've got to watch my butt while I'm in this country.

"Okay, nurse," Doman sighed, "let's cut this short; let her in."

I wanted Amelia to hear my answers just in case she was there under her father's orders.

She came in and forced a smile. Detective Litvack sucked in his gut. I caught the cops look, and I couldn't blame them, her skirt was very short.

It was the first time that I had seen her in daylight, and I felt flattered that such a beautiful, young woman was there to see me.

"Aren't you going to introduce the lady?"

"No."

"Well, it doesn't really matter, Mr. Swager. It looks like

we found the mysterious witness who came with you in the ambulance."

Amelia didn't bother to look at them but gave Litvack a little smirk as he resumed questioning me.

"What are you doing in Buffalo, Mr. Swager?"

"That's not relevant, nor is it any of your business. Even foreigners have legal rights and are entitled to a reasonable amount of privacy unless of course, you suspect I shot myself."

"Mr. Swager, your reasoning is a bit off. Whatever we ask is relevant. You can be assured that we will not violate your rights. We are trying to keep you safe, and we don't suspect you of shooting yourself. The slug they dug out of your chest came from a rifle. We also have witnesses to the occurrence, this lady being a very important one."

"Then why are you treating me like I'm the criminal?"

"I'm sorry if we've given you that impression but we have to find who's responsible. You must realize that you won't be safe until we do."

"Maybe it's a case of mistaken identity?"

"We might have believed that if we hadn't found the note that lured you outside."

He moved right along with his questions. "Okay, what is your connection to the Mongoose?"

"I don't know anything about a mongoose. Don't those things do good work and kill snakes?"

"Okay, you want to play dumb fine. The MONGOOSE ... Don Galante."

The description of the old man was exactly right, but how did they know? I asked the nurse for some more water.

I needed time to think. Amelia reacted before the nurse had a chance. She raised my head so I could drink, and when I was finished, she reached over and pulled the pillow up behind me. Her breast touched my face. It was intentional because she smiled and looked right at me. She was flirting, determined not to give up her quest to conquer my heart.

"Please, Mr. Swager, tell us what is your connection with Galante?"

"Well ... his daughter is a friend of mine."

"You and the kid of the Mongoose are an item?"

"I didn't say that. All I said was that we are friends."

I looked lovingly at Amelia as she kissed my forehead.

"You mean this is Galante's daughter? You said that she is your lawyer."

"You're getting better, detective. She is Amelia Galante, my counsel, and friend."

"I didn't know that she was a member of the bar. I thought that Ivan Rosenbluth represented the family."

"I don't know nor do I care about Rosenbluth. I know no one else in the Galante family but Amelia. As I understand it, I have the right to choose anyone to represent me, member of the bar or not."

Amelia's presence must have made them uneasy because they beat a hasty retreat, with the promise to continue their questioning when I felt better. I breathed a sigh of relief. They didn't seem to suspect me of anything illegal. They made no mention of drugs. However, it was unsettling that they knew about my dealings with Galante.

The nurse told Amelia that she could only stay a few

minutes and left the room. She caressed my cheek. She looked even more beautiful than the first time I had seen her. She ran her fingers through my hair, and she wasn't smiling when she said.

"It wasn't my family, Mickey. They would never put me in such a spot, and there is nothing in this world that could make me hurt you. I'd rather die than have you believe me responsible."

"This isn't about you; it's about me. Ultimately, your old man is responsible. He instigated the shipment, took advantage of me as I see it. He is ultimately responsible for the slug in my heart, no matter who pulled the trigger."

"Daddy didn't do this; I know it."

She saw I was going to say more, but she put a finger over my lips and kissed my forehead.

"How did Rojas get to pick me, I didn't even know the toad?"

"I don't know," she said as she wiped her tears. "He has his own people to look after that. He is most untrusting, and he insisted on using you, or the deal was off. All I did was check you out for our own protection because, in turn, dad doesn't trust Rojas. "

The door swung open:

"Sorry miss, you'll have to go now, time's up."

Amelia didn't move away but turned to look at who dared to bark orders at her.

"Get the hell out and stay out until I say so," she snarled.

The nurse first looked flustered, then angry, but she left, and a stranger took her place in the doorway.

"You need me, ma'am?"

"No Gino, it's okay; all's tight."

"Yes ma'am," he mumbled and left.

"Who the hell was that?"

"Mario has one of his guys watching your room."

"And who the hell is Mario?"

"My brother, half-brother."

"Oh yeah, I remember you talking about him Jesus ... Christ! I want this guy gone; your family has done me enough favors. That's probably how the cops connected me to your family."

"I'm sorry, it isn't my fault. I can't make him leave, even if I want to. He only takes orders from Mario. Besides, how do you know that the hit-man isn't coming back to take another crack at you, huh ...? Just tell me. How do you know? His being here also proves my family's innocence. Why else would we have a guy out in the hall."

"I don't know; this whole damn thing is too bizarre. I don't know of anyone ..."

"Anyone what ... you think you know who it is, don't you? You were ready to blame daddy and me, but you now know it isn't either of us. You were lured outside by a note the cops found. Why else would you have gone back out that door? It sure as hell wasn't to see me."

"No, it wasn't. I went out to get some fresh air."

"Oh yeah? That's a bunch of crap! You could see the car from the lobby. You were set up, and I've got a feeling you know by now by whom."

"Christ! There you go again jumping to conclusions. I'll

be glad when this is over, and I can go home. Why don't you just leave me alone."

She looked at me with a defiant expression and ignored what I'd said.

"Okay, does it have anything to with your trip to Brazil?"

"You know I went there?"

"Sure I know. I also know that you left in a hurry and didn't buy any logs. When I check someone out, I am exceedingly thorough. I don't stop at nothing."

"Anything."

"What?"

"Anything, I don't stop at nothing is a double negative."

"God almighty! I can't believe what I'm hearing. Here you are lying half-dead, and you're giving me friggin English lessons. Are you nuts or what?"

It was my turn to ignore her as she babbled on about my mental state. I thought back about my trip to Brazil. I knew Juan wouldn't talk, but other people had seen me there. Amelia's statement only proved how difficult it was to successfully cover any trail.

"Yeah … you finally see me for what I am. Nuts, got to be nuts, crazy like a loon because the sexiest, most beautiful girl that I have ever seen wants me, and I'm running like hell to get away from her."

"Oh, come on, you know that I didn't mean it that way."

"But I do. So just stay the hell away from me! I don't need you complicating my life with your teenage infatuation!"

"It's not infatuation! You can't dismiss me so easily, and

you can't say how I feel. You aren't in any position to judge my feelings!"

"You're probably right, but try to see things my way. I was dragged into this mess, and I want to get out fast, preferably alive. I'm not interested in a relationship with you. Because being around you is courting disaster."

"There is more to your story, Mickey. You're not completely honest. I saw you blow Louie away, remember? Uh uh ... you don't scare easy. You aren't afraid of my family or anything like that. I was very careful when I checked you out. You can handle yourself. There seems to be only one thing that scares you?"

"I shouldn't ask but I will anyway, what?"

"A relationship with a woman, now, that scares the crap out of you."

"Bull ... shit, lady!

"No, not bullshit. I'm going to find out who's out to get you."

"Oh, for Christ sake! You say that you love me and in the same breath, you're telling me that you're going to spy on me. Ha! I always believed the first rule of love is trust."

"I trust you, Mickey, but I don't trust your enemies and lying in this bed is proof enough that you have some. I'm not checking things out because I don't trust you, I'm checking them out because we have to be one step ahead of whoever wants you dead."

Seeing her determination, I realized that she meant business. She didn't know how close she had come to the truth about my enemies. After kissing my cheek and tightening the bow around her ponytail, she walked away. Gino got up when she opened the door and lowered his eyes when she passed by him, he too could appreciate a pair of nice legs.

"You can get your butt in there now, nursie."

She watched the nurse go into the room and left. It was a done deal for her; she knew that she wanted me and she wasn't going to let anything interfere with her plans.

A few days before I was discharged, the two cops came back with the picture of a man they had found dead in a hotel room. Before they had a chance to start questioning me, Detective Litvack nudged his partner, and they both looked towards the door, where a somber-looking, middle-aged man stood beside Gino.

"It seems that the young lady isn't your only friend in the Galante family, Mr. Swager. Your previous statement was obviously incomplete or deliberately misleading. I suggest that you be a little more forthcoming with your answers from now on. Back to the man in this picture, judging by the weapon we found in his hotel room, we have concluded that he was a professional hit man. The bullet removed from your chest came from his rifle. Ballistic tests were conclusive. It is obvious to us now that you know more about this situation than you're willing to tell us.

"I'm sorry, Sergeant, but you seem to know everything already, so I have nothing to add."

"Yes, we do have most of the answers. The motive seems to be the only piece of the puzzle we don't have. Your assailant was a pro who sure as hell wouldn't just shoot someone randomly. Here, I'll leave you my card. Give me a call when you feel like talking. Oh, and by the way, don't feel safe with the Galante family on your side. They can be quite fickle with their loyalty."

They nervously eyed the two men in the hall as they left. The photograph they had shown me was of Moreno, lying in the morgue with a bullet hole in his forehead. After saving my life in Honduras, he had obviously been given new orders. Raimundo must have found out about his wife's indiscretion, and he knew exactly where to find the bandito who had seduced her.

Amelia motioned for Mario to come in. I was getting used to her doing things her way.

In came a heavy-set, muscular man with wavy hair graying at the temples. His flattened nose and facial scars were evidence of how hard he worked for his father. There was no resemblance to Amelia's fine features. He didn't even look like his father. He gave me the creeps. He was disturbed when I told him that the man in the photograph the police had shown me, was Moreno. I asked him.

"Didn't you know?"

Mario wasn't at all forthcoming.

"Didn't I know what?"

"Didn't you know that he worked for Rojas?"

He obviously didn't like to be questioned. He was finding it difficult to remain civil.

"No ... I didn't and to tell the truth I don't give a fuck. The dumb fuck had it coming. Dad wants you in one piece. What I wanna know is, why Ray wants to get rid of you. That's what I wanna know. Doesn't he trust you? He must have at one point, or he or he would never have wanted you to look after things for him. You had to know each other."

"No, I had never heard of him until that Lumber Company contacted me about the deal. I'm even more surprised than you that he tried to have me killed."

"Whatever! You're safe now. I'm taking Gino off of the job."

He took one more look at me, nodded to his sister and walked out without another word. She reached over to pull the pillow up behind me, but I stopped her. I already knew that trick. She bewitched me, but my attraction for her was strictly physical. I would have taken advantage of the opportunity, had she not been who she was. There was a soft side to her that she couldn't hide. I saw love in her eyes and remembered feeling that way about someone once back in the sanatorium. Taking advantage of it would have been easy.

My recovery was unusually quick. There was uncertainty and sadness in her voice when she told me, "you'll be out of here tomorrow, Mickey. The doctor said that you should stay close because he wants to monitor your condition a while longer. The bullet damaged your heart, pulmonary artery, and aorta."

"Holy shit! That's a three in one shot. All that damage from one tiny little bullet, isn't that amazing?"

"Don't joke about it."

"Well the doctor probably wants to keep collecting his fee for as long as he can, but I'm going home, we have plenty of good doctors in Canada."

"It would be better if you stayed. You don't have anyone

else to take care of you, and it will give me a chance to make up for some of the things that I am responsible for."

It was clear that she had spent a lot of time on finding out about my past. It wasn't logical, but then, the whole business had been a mystery from the get-go.

"Look, I have no intention of spending the next few weeks in a hotel, and I certainly don't need you running back and forth as my nursemaid. Let's make a clean break and go our separate ways, besides I have a business to run and I'm not as safe here as at home. It's dangerous for me to be on this side of the border."

"You're expecting another hit?"

"I'm not sure, but I do know that someone in Washington has it in for me."

"Why not come home with me?"

"No thanks, I'm not ready for that morgue ... You're obviously not listening to me are you?"

"I am, Mickey, and I know that I should have more pride, but you have no idea what it is like."

"Yeah, and I was never young."

"I didn't mean that ... I meant that you don't know what it feels like being in love and being rejected."

"Yeah, as I said, I was never young."

"What has that got anything to with it."

"I was in love once; I damn well know what it is like. The best way is to part as friends and get over it."

"Do you think that I'm too immature?"

"No, but you could be making a mistake you'll regret for the rest of your life."

"You've made yours; let me make mine. Am I that unattractive?"

"On the contrary, besides being very attractive, you seem to know what you want and go for it. I admire that. Not so long ago, I would have fallen head over heels in love with you, but I've learned that once you're truly in love, it doesn't go away like a bad cold, it can eat your heart out. I like you too much to cause you such unhappiness."

"If you know me, you must also know that after that statement I'm even more determined."

"Well ... lady, I ain't ever going to set foot in your old man's compound ... unless you stick that gun in my face again."

I regretted those words as soon as they were out of my mouth.

"That was a low blow Mickey; you know that I couldn't hurt you, not now."

"I'm sorry. It was a mean thing to say, but I can't go back to your old man's place, it is like a morgue, for shit's sake."

"In other words, you would let me take care of you if it were somewhere else?"

"I hate hotels; you should know that by now."

"The estate was my home but hasn't been for over a year. I got my own apartment when I turned 21."

"Your family is letting you live away from your old man's home?"

"They know that no one would dare touch me. Boys were always afraid to ask me out. I thought that it would be different if I moved away but it hasn't changed a thing. The name Galante is enough to keep anyone away."

"So, you pick on this poor smuck because I'm older and dare to speak up to your old man. I almost believed that you liked me, but now I know you're just lonely."

"Yes, the fact that you're not afraid of dad means that you have guts, but that alone couldn't make me love you. I was infatuated with you before I met you. At least I thought it was infatuation, but I'm not so sure anymore. I have never felt this way about anyone, Mickey. I love you."

"But, I don't love you. You are very beautiful. You are very attractive, but I see no love in that. Attraction is not love and being around you won't change that."

"I could say that I understand, but I don't. You mean too much to me to let you walk away. I might never see you again. Besides, you've got to be realistic. The doctor here knows your case, so it is better to stay, at least for a while."

"I don't think it's wise. It will be even harder for you, a in couple of weeks from now, if what you feel is indeed love. The sooner I get away the better. Believe me, I know."

"How do you know that someone else isn't coming to finish the job?"

"I don't, but staying with you in Buffalo doesn't guarantee that they won't try again."

"I know, but I'm licensed to carry a gun. In Canada, you'd be a sitting duck."

"I see your point, but you have to understand that it wouldn't be easy for you seeing me day after day.

"I know that you don't love me, Mickey. Even if something

happened between us, what would be the harm? I know what I'm doing. I'm going into this with my eyes wide open."

"Even though you know that I don't love you?"

"I'll take all I can get, no regrets. Sure I would like you to love me but if it doesn't happen, so be it. Just being around you makes me happy."

She scanned my face for some sign of giving in and accepting her offer.

"There would have to be some rules."

"Anything, as long as you say yes."

"Okay. You have to promise me that you won't try to keep me here when I have to go."

"I promise."

"What about your family?"

"What about them?"

"Don't they care about someone my age and background living with you?"

"No, they respect my privacy."

We had an agreement. I saw that she had a hard time controlling her emotions. I couldn't help but wonder if I had made the right decision.

Her apartment was comfortable. She had chosen to decorate it simple, in direct contrast to the mortuary decor of her father's home. The windows had blinds not velvet curtains. Her bookcase was made of bricks and planks. The floor was hardwood with a large bearskin rug in front of the fireplace. The whole place was light and modern, yet cozy. Sharing her living space wouldn't be a sacrifice. It felt like home the moment I entered. She kept her promise and didn't mention her feelings even though they were obvious. Being around her was also having its effect on my honorable intentions. Cold showers became less effective, it didn't help that she wore even shorter skirts at home than those she wore when she went out. Although my wounds were now healed and I had been given the green light by the doctor to travel, she always found a reason for me to stay. Admittedly, it didn't take too much persuasion.

One particular evening, a warm fire, a bottle of wine and a howling wind made her place a real haven. Uncharacteristically, I had one glass of wine too many and got to talking about my past. I told her about my relationship with Maggie but left out the real reason for our splitting up. I wasn't yet ready to confess to that crime. I knew that there is no statute of limitations on murder. Amelia had done me a favor making me look back. She was right calling me cynical and distrustful of women. I hadn't planned to tell her my life story, but I wanted her to know who I was. Maybe she would stop digging if she knew enough.

She looked angry, and staring into the fire she said, "if I ever see that bitch, I'll kill her."

"Don't talk like a kid, this stuff about killing doesn't suit you. It may impress your family but not me."

"I love you, Danny."

"Yeah ... I gathered as much. But we agreed not to go into that subject. I happen to believe that nothing in this world is free. Not even love, one or the other will have to pay the price for the privilege eventually."

"I want to live with you, and I gladly pay the price."

"Well ... isn't that what we are doing?"

"You know what I mean."

"I do, but don't get your hopes up. You're young, and there's a whole world out there that you haven't even begun to explore. You may think that you know a lot, but when I hear you talk the way you just did, it just affirms how young you are. Trust me when I say that. I'm not trying to hurt you. Maggie and I happened when I was about your age and look what it has done to me. I still have that boyish romantic impression of her because I never knew her any other way. Hell ... maybe if I saw her today I wouldn't even bother taking another look ... who knows."

"Don't compare me to you. Times were different; you were different. Being in that joint must have been very hard. The way I see it, she took advantage of you when you were very vulnerable."

"You're probably right but she made me feel like a man, and she was there when I needed someone."

"But she also left you when you needed her. Let's face it; she cared more about herself than about you."

"Maybe but the memories are all I have ... Anyway, it isn't any of your business. I think that you should concentrate on people your own age. Besides, I am not exactly who you think I am. I have done things that I'm not very proud of."

"What? Blowing Louie away? He whacked some people himself; it shouldn't bother you. Sometimes you have no choice if you want to survive. You can't go around doing penance for the rest of your life."

"That doesn't change the way I feel about myself."

"Wow … wow … just a minute, what am I missing here; let's back up for a second. Are you saying that you don't think that you're good enough for me?"

"I guess … but it isn't just that. It wouldn't be fair to string you along when I am still hung up on someone else."

"Damn, I know that! I understand how you feel about her. Why can't you understand how I feel about you? She didn't care about you, and you still love her after all those years."

"I … I don't know. Probably."

"Don't you feel attracted to me at all?"

"More than you know, I'm very attracted to you, and I am fighting like hell to do the right thing because I respect you; I'd be a liar to deny it."

"You tell me this now?"

"Yeah."

"You could've told me this a long time ago. I thought that you didn't like the way I am or looked down on me because of my family. I thought …"

"No, it isn't you; it's me! I admit that I was afraid of getting involved because of your family but not anymore. I just don't want to feel like a rat when I go home."

"Let me get this straight. You don't want to make love to me because it might make you feel like a rat. I am not as fragile as you think. I want you without any strings attached. I have already said that I will get you eventually, but that doesn't mean that I will try to keep you against your will. You're still free to leave whenever you want. Maybe you're more concerned about your own feelings than mine."

"Could be … but there's more."

"More what, true confessions?"

"Yes, more confessions. I've been with other women since Maggie."

"How often, once twice, a hundred times or what?"

"No … a few times; other times I would have liked to but I was always afraid of getting too involved."

"You're 34 years old for God's sake, and nobody could expect you to live like a monk. Get it through your thick head that I don't scare easy."

She stared at me. Her eyes moistened and glistened with light from the fireplace. She stood up and moved her pile of cushions closer to mine. Her short skirt left just enough to the imagination as she bent over. She stood before me as I ran my hand up her leg and under her skirt. She smiled and knelt down beside me. I took her in my arms and kissed her for the first time. I knew I'd lost my battle and carried her to the bedroom where we made love. When it was over, we held each other for a long time. She finally said with a sigh, "Oh, Mickey, I have wanted you since the first time I saw you."

She was wonderful. Somehow, I couldn't get the feeling that I was taking advantage of her, out of my mind. I felt the lust and the satisfaction but there was still something missing and whatever it was, was enough to keep me from completely committing myself to her. She was oblivious to my concerns, and when I tried to get up, she held me tighter.

"No, Mickey, don't go yet. I might never be this happy again. I didn't know how much I loved or wanted you until now. Stay a while and hold me. I know that I led you on, but

I will only have the memory when you're gone, and I'm going to make it last as long as I can. Deep down, I worried that I might be disappointed."

"Then you weren't."

"No, Mickey, of course, I wasn't."

"I was afraid that I might have been too rough and I didn't want to hurt you."

"No, I had heard that the first time always hurts a woman, but it didn't."

We lay in each other's arms, her head was under my chin, and I remembered how it was for my first time. We made love again and again until we fell asleep just before dawn.

She became more attached to me in the days that followed. I knew it was time to go. The longer I waited, the harder it would be for me, as well as for her. I was afraid that I was falling in love and I couldn't let that happen. Besides my business was suffering, even though my partner was more than capable to keep it afloat.

It was a warm afternoon, and we sat in the park for the last time. Fall was in the air, and I was going home. Reluctant to let me go, she couldn't hide her sadness. An old man sitting on a bench across from us had a large flock of pigeons gathered around him. I had seen him there before; it was his daily routine. He smiled while the birds shoved, pushed and flapped their wings to get their fair share of the food. When the bag was empty, he blew it full of air and twisted the top closed. The birds suspected nothing and went about finding the last of the seeds amongst the fallen leaves. Looking at me, he winked with a sly grin. He slammed his hands together popping the bag. Amelia jumped as the pigeons flew up in a big cloud of feathers and wings. They came back almost immediately as if that was what the old man wanted from them in return for the food. His fun was over, and he left. Amelia watched him sauntering away.

"Old goat, somebody should scare the crap out of him."

"Yeah, old goat," I said, "that will be me in a few years, and I'll be looking at the young couple sitting across from me."

"Ooh ... stop the melodramatic crap, Mickey! It's not going to change the way I feel. I don't feel sorry for you. I feel sorry for myself. You'll go and find another girl. Maybe you will even find your old flame."

The pigeons had taken up their post on the fountain and waited for the next old man with a bag. We crossed the road, and a flock of noisy crows left a nearby tree. It reminded me of the day I'd left the San, and I remembered what Victoria had said about love. Amelia thought that she had found it, just as I had once. The way I had things figured out, love was a one-way street. Very few lucky ones find long-time happiness as a couple. I pictured Maggie beside me and no matter how hard I tried to see it differently; no one else seemed to fit the slot that was meant for her.

I left the following Monday and waved good-bye through the back window of the cab. She was true to her word and didn't stand in my way when it was time to leave, but I did see how she fought back the tears when we kissed good-bye. Even though I didn't like cities, Buffalo would always be OK because Amelia lived there and she would always have a place in my heart. She had almost made me forget about Maggie but not quite. I made the decision that I would have to see if I could find her and get things settled in my mind and my heart. She had taken too much from me. It was time to come to terms with myself, to be at peace, and perhaps have another chance at happiness, before I took my place with the paper bag on the park bench.

10

It stopped snowing, and the wind was dying down, but the battle in the streets was just beginning. Cars, trucks, and buses inched along. Pedestrians, with their faces buried in scarves and collars, kicked up the powdery snow in little puffs. The vendor across the street brushed off his papers and magazines, locked the kiosk and left with his lunch box under his arm. I watched the activity on the street below from the comfort of my office. Moaning and groaning snow-clearing equipment was coming closer. I stood in the dark, nursing my drink until the rush hour was finished. I used to like this city, but now, congested, polluted and noisy, it had lost its attraction, especially in the winter. There were times when I would have liked to move to a more temperate climate, but I had my business to run. I had been tempted to sell out, but I couldn't just stop working and do nothing. Trips to the tropical forests gave me a break in the long winter months, but now a mysterious enemy, south of the border had put a stop to that. Whatever I'd done to him wasn't going away. Killing

Savoy had not solved the problem; I remained vigilant. I often sensed that I was being watched but never actually saw anyone following me. Over the last few days the feeling had grown stronger, and he felt that it wouldn't be long before something was going to happen; I just didn't think it would be on this miserable, winter evening.

I heard something in the outer office and put the glass down on the window-sill. Joanne and the girls had left and locked the door as usual. That door was the only way in, and if one of them had come back, she would have turned the lights on. The door to the private office was closed but not locked. My heart started thumping, and I looked around for a weapon, grabbing my old baseball bat. The beam of a flashlight shone under the door as I moved quietly beside it, raising the bat as the doorknob turned. I held my breath. I first saw a gun barrel then a hand ... I brought the bat down on the wrist as hard as I could. There was a loud snap, the gun fell to the floor, and the intruder tumbled forward screaming in agony. I kicked the door shut and stood back waiting to see if he was alone. My intruder was on his knees, hunched over holding his wrist. He screamed and swore as I turned the lights on. The ends of broken bone sticking through the skin turned my stomach, but I felt no sympathy and quickly fished the gun out from under the desk

"For Christ's sake man, get me an ambulance," the man whimpered.

"Like hell. First, you talk, then we'll see about the ambulance."

"What talk? I went around trying doors, and this one was open."

"Yeah, right! You go around trying doors with a piece in your hand, just in case you run into the competition."

"No, for Christ sake; I found it on the last job, and I took it ... Goddamn it! Call a fucking ambulance. This hurts like a son-of-a-bitch!"

"Good, it may teach you to think twice about entering somewhere uninvited."

I handed him a towel from the washroom to stop him from bleeding all over the floor. He wrapped it around his wrist and held his arm. It was clear that the burglar wasn't there by chance and I figured the guy wouldn't talk to me anyway, so I stuck the gun in my belt and gave my guest a glass of scotch to keep him from passing out and then I called Ben.

Ben used to be a close friend of mine before I went into the sanatorium, but as time passed, he became more of an acquaintance. Ben was a private investigator. He worked mostly for banks and creditors, finding people trying to escape their financial obligations.

"Here, down this, it might help."

Sniffing it, he looked suspiciously but in obvious pain. He put the glass on the desk saying, "aren't you gonna have one?"

"No, I never touch the stuff."

He watched me pour myself a glass of Southern Comfort.

"How do I know that you didn't put something in my drink?"

"You don't."

"Why don't you give me some of what you're having?"

"Drink the scotch or leave it, I don't give a shit."

Sniffing the scotch again, he took a sip. Then gulped it down and held the glass out for more.

"Why are you giving me drinks?" he grunted after taking another gulp. "It isn't going to change what I told you."

"I know but you're drinking from the bottle that I keep here for the guy who is on his way over, he gets meaner than stink when I serve it to anyone else. I mean, mean enough to make Rambo talk."

"Who the fuck is Rambo?"

"Read Morrell's book, you idiot, although ... you're probably illiterate." Neither insult nor booze changed his painful expression but his complexion reddened as he rocked back and forth in the chair holding his arm. The snow had probably slowed Ben down; it took him a half-hour to arrive. He grabbed the bottle of scotch as soon as he came in. First, he looked to see how much was left, then at the man in obvious pain, still rocking in the chair.

"God-damn it, Mick, is he drinking my scotch?"

The visitor eyed him apprehensively, lifting his shoulder like a dog expecting to be hit.

"Yeah, ... it's your bottle all right."

"He bloody well better be worth it."

Probably not, but I had to give him something to keep him from passing out before you got here."

Ben was tall and muscular; one angry stare was usually enough to intimidate anyone looking for an argument. I gave him a glass. He filled it and looked at the man in the chair.

"Know who he is?"

"Nope, he's trying to tell me that he is a burglar who came here by chance but I doubt it. Here, this is what he came in with."

I gave him the gun. He looked it over, released the clip, looked at the bullets and shook his head. "These slugs are meant to kill. They mushroom and turn your guts into hamburger. He ain't no burglar, that's for sure. If he came looking for you, you're lucky that you came out ahead."

Ben took the towel from the man's wrist.

"Jesus Christ! What did you use on him, a wrecking bar?"

"No, my bat," I said pointing to the corner.

"Shit, sure glad it wasn't me carrying a piece."

"Aren't you?"

Ben didn't answer. I knew he had one strapped to his leg. He had several, one of them now on the bottom of the La Ceiba harbor, where I dumped it before leaving Honduras.

"My God, that must hurt."

The man grimaced but didn't answer as Ben threw the towel back over the shattered wrist.

"Perhaps we could do something about that arm if you told us a few things."

"Go to Hell," he said as he kept rocking.Ben grabbed him by the lapels of his coat and hoisted him out of the chair. He screamed like a pig in the slaughterhouse. Ben frisked him.

"Charles B. Douglas ... Shit, this guy works for the DEA. Are you messing with drugs Mick?"

Ben looked at Douglas and asked, "what are you doing here?"

He ignored the question and was shoved back in the chair, which almost tipped over and resulted in more cursing.

"I was hired to kill Swager!" he yelled.

"Why?"

"Fuck you! I'm not telling you nothing else."

He quickly got up when Ben made another move towards the chair.

"I don't know; I never met the guy who hired me. All I know is that he is a big-shot in DC."

The burglar didn't like the way the questions were asked, but who cared, it brought results. The Senator had tried very hard to keep his name out of it, but he had become more daring … or desperate.

Ben walked over to the chair and gave it another good kick. Douglas yelped again, "what the fuck was that for? I answered your goddamn questions!"

"That was a bonus for drinking my scotch."

I sensed that there was something missing from the story, Charlie Douglas talked too easily. It took much more to get information out of Savoy, yet they both worked for the same boss and presumably went through the same training. However, Douglas had told me all I needed to know, and it was time for the police to do the rest. The police station was only two blocks away, but they waited twenty minutes. They were compassionate enough not to handcuff the prisoner. The detectives who came in minutes later took our statements and asked me why Ben had been called before them.

"Don't know, I never had anybody break into my office

before. I guess I called him because … he's an old friend who knows more about this stuff than I do."

"Most people call the police first, why didn't you?"

"Let's face it guys. You're not all that good, if you were, we wouldn't have scum like him trying to rob or kill us."

"That, my friend, is the stupidest thing I've ever heard.

"Fine … then get your ass out of my office and take that garbage with you; I'm not the criminal, hassle him."

"You'll sing a different tune when you need us, chum."

They left in a huff. I knew I was unreasonable, but I couldn't think of anything else to say at the time. Ben sat in his chair and grinned, nursing another scotch.

"Put the glass down for a moment, Ben, we have to talk. Something bothers me about Douglas. I had a tiff with one of those guys in Brazil, and it took a hell of a lot more to make him talk. Those bastards are tough; they can handle pain and not talk."

"What makes you think that he was hiding something?"

"As I said, he talked too easily."

"Maybe he isn't a real DEA agent. Maybe he is a guy who works for himself."

"Yeah, could be. I just have the feeling that his visit here was to tie up some loose ends. If he wanted to kill me, he wouldn't come to my office when I wasn't likely to be here."

"Why *does* someone want you out of the way?"

"Can't tell you everything, but I can tell you this. The big-shot in DC is a Senator. He sent a hit-man after me in Brazil, I don't know why … I have been racking my brain trying to figure it out but haven't come up with anything."

"Hm … the guy in Brazil … you came out ahead considering you're here."

"Yeah."

"Kill him?"

"That's none of your business, besides it doesn't make any difference."

"If you want my help, you'd better come clean now; I don't want any surprises blowing up in my face."

"Look, Ben, you're not a lawyer and by no means a priest. There is no law in Canada for client privilege as far as PIs are concerned. It could be *you* blowing up in *my* face. You could be forced to repeat anything I say in court. I'll tell you all I can but if you don't feel comfortable, hey … I'll have no option but to shop for someone else. I understand your concerns, but my life is on the line, and I'm not about to blow it because you can't handle the risk."

"Whoa … whoa, don't get on your high horse. I didn't say that I wouldn't or couldn't. You know I won't let you down; we're friends for Christ sake!"

"You've got that almost right. We were friends until I got put in the San. Where were my friends then? They disappeared like I had the plague"

"GODDAMNIT … You won't let me forget it, will you? You know that my parents forbade me from having anything to do with you. We were kids for Christ sake! You know that, and you still hold it against me."

"Well … yeah … I guess I've still got some problems to work out … want the job?"

"Hell, yeah … I can't blame you for feeling the way you

do. Maybe I should have told my old man to shove it. I know how hard it was for you alone out there."

"Like shit you do ... you don't know anything about that crap."

"No ... not for a long time because you never want to talk about it, but I met a buddy of yours. He said he knew you from there and told me all about it."

"Well, that was a long time ago ... what was his name?"

"Christ ... what the hell was his name. I met him in a bar on Crescent Street ... it started with an S ... Saline ... Salter, Sullivan ... shit, I forgot. It was a while ago, as a matter of fact, it was sometime before you went to Brazil."

"Savoy?"

"Yeah, that's it, Savoy ... remember him? Tall guy with long blond hair, about our age."

"Yeah I remember him, he's dead now."

"I'm sorry ... shit, he looked so healthy. I thought that people didn't get TB anymore."

"He *was* healthy, never had TB, as far as I know. He wasn't with me in the San. He fed you that crap because he wanted to find out about me. He pumped you for information, and you fell for it like a rookie and set me up for a hit."

Ben fell silent; he should have known that Savoy was interrogating him. He used the same tactics himself.

"Christ ... I'm sorry, Mick. I ... I didn't know. Is he the guy from Brazil?"

"Can't tell you because that's where things get kind of sticky, but I do know that I'm in a hell of a mess."

Ben suddenly stood up and motioned me to keep quiet.

He took his coat and was about to leave without finishing his drink; it wasn't like him. I was about to say something, but again he motioned to be quiet and pointed at the walls and then his ears. I got the message and followed him out locking the door.

"Look," Ben said. "From what you are telling me we can expect anything including bugs planted here and in your pad. We'll go to my office and get my bag of tricks; then we'll go and check out your place. Tomorrow we'll check your office. Those fucking things can be hidden anywhere."

I waited in the car while Ben went into his office for his bag. He had mentioned the bag before, and I was about to find out what he kept in it. He came back to the car with a briefcase and tossed it on the back seat.

"Is that the famous bag?"

"Yeah, paid a lot of bucks for the last gadget, let's see if it was worth the dough."

"What gadget?"

"A tiny camera that goes in small places and around corners; it's an experimental one in fiber optics or something. I've played with it but never actually used it on a job."

It was about ten o'clock when we parked the car. Ben suggested that I wait until he was finished checking the garage. From there we went upstairs. I was about to put the key in the lock when Ben grabbed my arm and pulled me back.

"Hey, there are lights on for Christ sake, I can see it under the door."

"Yeah, I know they are on a timer. I hate coming home to the dark."

Ben checked the edges and the lock but found nothing. He unlocked the door and opened it slightly. Then he took something that looked like a piece of black cable and slipped it under the door and connected it to a small monitor. A moment or so later he cursed, "h-o-l-y shit!"

"What?"

"It looks like the door is booby-trapped. I can see what looks like shotgun tied to a chair, pointing at the door. So that's why Charlie Douglas talked so easily."

"Okay, now what, can we de-activate it?"

"No, too dangerous."

"Can't you do something?"

"Yeah sure, but not de-activate it. I'll have to blow it."

"What about the bomb squad?"

"Well, it looks like it's a booby trap, but I can't be sure. We'll look damn stupid if it is nothing but a prank."

"What do you mean a prank? Somebody got into my place to set this up for shit sake. That's not a prank to me."

"Obviously, but it could be something just to scare you. You'll be asked a lot of questions."

"Like?"

"Like how you suspected that there was something fishy here. Secondly, remember the way you talked to them earlier tonight?"

"Yeah, you're probably right, but I'll be asked those questions anyway. What the hell ... go for it, blow the sucker."

Ben lay flat on his stomach beside the door. I watched from the end of the hall. Ben looked back to make sure that I was out of the way and nobody else was around, and then he gave the door a push. The shotgun blast cut the door practically in half. I shuddered. Ben brushed the debris from his clothing while we stepped over the junk and had a look at the offending contraption. I felt myself shaking. Neighbors in dressing gowns and pajamas gathered in the hall. The kick had dislodged the shotgun and thrown it behind the couch on the other side of the room. The stench of cordite accompanied the blue haze that filled the room. Ben had made a quick tour before the police got there.

"So we meet again ... eh, Swager! It looks like you'd better tell me what the hell is going on. Twice in one night is more than acceptable to us, underpaid and under qualified slugs. Oh yeah, ... we found out that the DEA is after you. Agent Douglas talked."

"That's great work detective. Talk to him some more and enlighten me because I sure as hell don't know what is going on."

"I see your PI friend still with you. It leads me to believe that you know a lot more than you're willing to tell me."

"That friend just saved my ass, if it weren't for him, you'd be here with the coroner on a homicide investigation."

"If you'd talked to us, you'd still have a door. You suspected something and called your buddy instead of us. The bomb squad could have dismantled the device and help us solve the case. As it stands now ... all we have is dust."

He stepped over the garbage, shaking his head with the forensic team behind him. They started blowing the dust from the various items and replaced it with their own brand.

Ben offered to have me bunk in with him, but I knew his

habit of heavy drinking at the end of the day, when he was relaxed, as he defined it. At that stage he often became argumentative, so I thanked him and stayed at a hotel instead.

Things were calm after the shotgun incident; there were no further attempts on my life, but it would only be a matter of time before another, possibly successful attempt. The police bothered me for a while but eventually gave it up as another unsolved case.

A couple of weeks went by, and I received a request to testify at some hearings in Washington, concerning the trafficking of illegal substances. Could it be that they were interested in my his dealings with the Galante family? McBain was chairman of the committee making it clear that it was simply a ploy to get me back within his jurisdiction. This was an unexpected change in his tactics. The Senator had originally wanted me dead and buried in Brazil. When that failed, he tried again, unsuccessfully in Montreal. Why, did he want to find out how much I knew? Was he getting impatient? Perhaps he wasn't as informed about me as he thought he was. Going to Washington might be a good opportunity to find the answers to what I wanted to know. The Senator obviously had a lot of influence if he could set up hearings just to get to me, or was it an opportunity where hearings were already planned long ago?

I declined the invitation because there were no guarantees that I wouldn't be arrested on some trumped up charge. This didn't stop McBain. He then tried to have me extradited. Not convicted or indicted for any crime in the US, extradition would be difficult to justify.

The extradition attempt failed. McBain wouldn't be able to hold up the hearings to wait for my arrival. I wanted to get things settled as well and hired a lawyer to work out the details involved to go voluntarily. A showdown was inevitable, and it would be safer in Washington. I demanded full immunity before crossing the border.

An invitation from Don Galante to spend some time at the family estate came as no surprise. I knew the Don was keeping an eye on me. He probably wanted to discuss his own impending testimony. I thanked him and declined the invitation. I didn't care much for the family nor the estate, and my last visit was too memorable. My business with him was finished; I wasn't interested in any new ventures with him. I thought I had made that clear the evening I had been kidnapped.

Two weeks later a telephone call from the Don left me no recourse but to meet with him. He was staying at the Windsor Hotel in Montreal. Something more important than assuring My silence must have been on his mind. It was rare for him to leave his home. If it had been that only, his son could have been adequately intimidating.

Gino and another man stood guard in the hall, and he was about to frisk me when the old man opened the door. When he saw me standing spread-eagle against the wall, he said in a voice raspier than I remembered.

"Don't touch that man. He is a respected guest and a personal friend of mine."

Gino jumped back and looked sheepishly. I couldn't pass up an opportunity to take a shot at him.

"My ... my, Gino," I smiled. You are advancing fast in your career. From geek to goon in a matter of months, all before finishing grade school."

He clenched both his teeth and his fists. His little twitches were evidence of his anger. I followed the Don into the suite and remained standing. Manners were very important to him.

"That wasn't fair, Swager. You know that he is no match for you."

"Then why do you have people like him working for you?"

"Because people like you won't."

"Knowing that you shouldn't have come."

"That's not why I'm here. Sit, and I will explain why it was necessary for me to travel even under my difficult circumstances."

He rang a little bell standing on the table beside him; a young man came in. He brought a tray with a bottle and some glasses, poured us both a drink and left the room without saying anything. Much to my surprise, it was a bottle of Southern Comfort. The Don had a good memory, and I was flattered by the gesture.

"I'd like to make this short and sweet, Swager. I had you thoroughly investigated, by Amelia, before you looked after that cargo for me. Someone else has kept me posted since you left Buffalo because Amelia doesn't want to be involved in the day to day operations of the business. The reports I have on you, my intuition and my understanding of people, tell me that you are a man of honor. You are courageous, honest and you have integrity ... I left diplomatic off the list considering what you said to Gino."

He hesitated.

"Don Galante, we both know that you didn't come here just to pay me a compliment."

He stared at me for a moment. It was one of his stares that gave me chills.

"No Swager, you are also insolent, but I'm putting that aside for the moment. My daughter has been very distraught since you left Buffalo. I understand that she is in love with you. She has changed, and I rarely see her anymore. You are partly to blame for that. The two of you meeting was a regrettable mistake. I would have wanted her to get to know someone of Italian descent, but love is a strange phenomenon ... I would be very proud to have you as a member of my family."

"But Don Galante, I thought that I made it clear ..."

He stopped me by raising his hand.

"No young man, I know what you are thinking, not into the business, especially not into "the family business." You would make beautiful grandchildren. I would like at least one before I die."

I started to object, but the wedding was already a fait acompli. He stopped me and gave me that stare, again

"I know that you will be faithful to her and that you will keep her, as well as yourself, out of the business. It is obvious that you don't love her the way she loves you, but that will come in time. Regardless of what you think, I'm telling you that she has no blood on her hands and I know you will keep it that way. This marriage will benefit you. You will get one million dollars as soon as you announce your engagement and another million on the day of the wedding; consider it a dowry."

He put down the glass, his cigar, and sat with open arms looking at me as if he were expecting me to kneel for his blessing. I stood and walked over to the window. Galante was trying to tell me that he was dying and obviously he wanted things settled before he did.

"Look, son, you don't have to give me an answer right now, although that would be nice. After your business in Washington is finished, perhaps we can talk again."

I wasn't sure how much he knew, but I suspected his investigator to be very thorough. Alphonse Galante was an old son-of-a-bitch, but he was the father of a girl I cared about. With all his experience in life, I wondered why he couldn't see that the acceptance of this proposal would make me the exact opposite of what he believed me to be. The money was attractive, but the way I would have come by it would be worse than robbery. I had to face him with the answer, no matter how uncomfortable.

"Don Galante, I would be no more than a whore, not worthy of your daughter, if I accepted your offer. She is one of the finest women I know. I have thought about marrying her, but never for money. I can only marry for love, and I don't love her enough. True love is what your daughter deserves; anything less is unacceptable. Is that what you want for her?"

The Don sat in the chair, his shoulders drooped. Pulling a handkerchief from his pocket, he blew his nose. His drink forgotten and the Cuban cigar was burning away in the ashtray. He spoke, without looking at me as if he were ashamed of his tears ... or the proposal ... or perhaps both.

"The poor immigrant boy from Verona built an empire worth millions, but he can't get his daughter the man she wants. Look, Micky, I didn't love my wife when we married but it came eventually, it will for you too if you feel the way you do now. My wife died, but she still lives on in my heart and through my daughter."

It was the first time he had called me Mickey.

"I am truly sorry, Don Galante, marriage for me is a one-time deal and I wouldn't gamble my, or Amelia's happiness on anything less than a sure thing. If she is unhappy now, it will pass. If we married and she were unhappy, it would be forever.

"Tell me, Mickey, is it I who brought this on her, is it the business?"

I should have felt honored by the question. He was the Don, and he was supposed to have all the answers.

"Don Galante, neither you nor the family business has anything to do with it. I know that she would marry me regardless of how I feel about her. I could never wake up with her beside me knowing that I did not love her, she deserves to be loved."

"I understand Mickey; it is the integrity I was talking about, that is why I want you for her. If you agreed, you are right; you wouldn't be who you are. It is a lose-lose situation for me ... I should never have come."

I left him with his thoughts. I realized that I'd treated Amelia badly by leaving her and not calling her ... not even once.

11

It was spring, and young lovers were back in the city parks. My thoughts weren't about spring but about the negotiations for my trip to Washington. I'd agreed to attend if I were accorded full immunity and safe conduct. The Senator didn't have much choice but to agree. He was running out of time. If the hearings ended before I appeared, he would have to find another way of getting to me, and if I didn't go, I would never know why McBain had a beef with me. There was a better chance of finding out more about this mystery by facing him. It was imperative that I be better informed before going to Washington. For that, I needed to research my past. The first thing that could be considered a turning point in my life was my time at the sanatorium. Before that, I had been too sheltered and innocent. The most likely event was the Rodriguez affair. Perhaps he had a distant relative or a friend of McBain. Although, if that were the case, he could have gone through official channels and not sent a killer. I had never heard about the discovery of a body in Ste. Agathe but it could have happened during one of my trips out of the country when I didn't stay abreast of local news, that possibility made the library my priority. I carefully listed my travel dates from my records. It would help to narrow my search. It took me three days to scan the past 13 years with no results. Could it be that the body had been found and the discovery had been kept a secret to avoid tipping-off the murderer? I dreaded the thought of going back there, but if the body were still there, I'd still be safe. If however, it were gone, an open case file would still be on someone's desk. I was reluctant to even be in the area.

I started out early in the morning. I entered and exited the expressway on two separate occasions I arrived in Ste. Agathe mid-morning. There were quite a few changes, but that was to be expected I hoped that the town's expansion hadn't spread as far as the old chalet and the ravine with the dumpsite. The road to the sanatorium hadn't changed. There were a few more houses and another gas station. I drove up to the sanatorium. It looked worse than I remembered. The grounds were unkempt and the surrounding woods untouched. The screening around the balconies was still there, but it was torn and rusted. It was hard to imagine that I had once called this home. I had promised myself never to return, but I was back; so were the memories and faces flashed by ...

A young woman who went to Montreal for her surgery. Four weeks later she was back, distraught and scarred for life. Someone had discovered she was pregnant after she was on the operating table with her ribs spread apart. The surgery was stopped immediately.

Pierre Gamache vomiting and pale, he was desperate because the doctor had told him that part of his left lung had to be removed. His right had been taken the year before. The doctor apologized hours later for the mix-up in the X-rays, but Pierre had gone through hell for a while. What had happened to nurse Tang? Maggie? All those others? What had happened to all the wheezing orderlies? It was common knowledge that administrators kept patients longer than necessary, to keep their cushy jobs in the resort area. They had obviously, eventually failed. Now the doors and windows were boarded up. The graffiti artists had been as busy here as in the city. Tufts of grass in the cracks of the pavement were competing with the dandelions. The San stood there, just like any other abandoned building. I had been 21 when I was released, but now I was 34. Nothing had "REALLY" changed with me. I still worried about a relapse whenever I had a cold or felt under the weather. My experience with Maggie had made me hesitant about entering into any relationship. Perhaps, I used her as an excuse to be distrustful of other women or was it simply an excuse to wallow in self-pity? I'd learned to live for myself, sharing nothing, be it pain, love or joy. My only hope for a normal life was to find Maggie and settle things once and for all. People usually move on after a breakup. I hadn't, perhaps, because it had happened at such a critical time in my life. Regardless of the reasons or excuses. I looked toward the path I had walked that disastrous day so many Junes ago. I was tempted to see if the chalet was still there, but that wasn't why I had come. I left feeling more depressed and drove down the road to find the Whispering

Pines Motel. The sign was gone. Only the post was left. It was unlikely that Gepetto and his wife were still alive, but someone else could be living there. The driveway didn't look as if it were used anymore but that didn't mean anything, with all the changes in the area, there could be a new driveway.

I drove on a little further and pulled up on the shoulder. The brush was so thick in places that it didn't seem as if there had ever been a driveway. When I reached the clearing, I stood for a moment and listened. The pines still whispered. The trees smelled the same, and the air was still clear and fresh. There were only remnants of the main house; it had apparently burned to the ground, but the blackened brick chimney still stood. Perhaps Gepetto had lit one cigarette too many? The cabins lay in ruins. The one where Maggie and I had once stayed had all but vanished. Only the floor was left. Rotting wood was strewn about. Grass and weeds had pushed through the cracks of the floor. Soon all evidence of it would be buried under rotting leaves, pine needles and weeds. It began to dawn on me how long it had been. Thinking back, it felt as if it were only yesterday. I had been happy then. I closed my eyes and saw her. She had come with love, hope, and happiness, taking away my despair and loneliness, bringing joy and meaning to my life. Then she had taken it all away leaving nothing. After all these years, I realized how much I missed her and how empty my life was.

I left the clearing and went into the bush to find the ravine wall. It wasn't far, but it took time to reach because the bush had grown so much and the trees were so much taller. The new foliage, however, was lacey and frail. It gave me less cover than I would have liked I had to finish what I started. I made my way along the steep embankment. I stepped on some metal beneath the grass and leaves, recognizing it as a piece of the same galvanized roofing that I'd used to cover the body. I knew that I was close. My heart raced when I saw what was left of the mattress. The rusty metal springs were protruding. Much of the fabric and padding had disintegrated. I hesitated, afraid to look at what was left of the corpse, but more afraid to find nothing at all. I clenched my teeth and grabbed the edge of the sheet metal. Weeds and saplings had grown through the holes and around the edges holding it firmly down as if wanting to guard its secret. My heart was pounding as I managed to lift the junk high enough to see underneath. I breathed a sigh of relief when I saw a skeleton. The skull was turned sideways, just the way I'd left him. Most of the clothing was still evident. He appeared to grin, and I shivered. I let the metal fall back and ran, afraid to get too caught up in the past. I hadn't come to be sentimental. I needed facts, and one fact was that my problems didn't come from what had happened fifteen years ago.

Back in the car, I felt more relaxed. It was over; my secret was still safe. I stopped the car at the top of the hill to look at the town in the valley behind me. I knew now that it should never have taken me so long to make up my mind to find Maggie. I had financial security and time. I could have tried long ago and hadn't. Now strange as it seemed, I was grateful to the Senator.

12

It was an ominous feeling being in Washington. I watched the people while standing against the wall at the back of the room. There were few cameras present. It probably wasn't a newsworthy event. A teenage girl passed me and looked at me curiously for a moment and sat down. I watched my attorney getting ready. It took my thoughts back to Buffalo. I had found myself thinking of Amelia more often since her father had died. She had made more of an impact on me than I cared to admit. The attraction wasn't just sexual; she had become a friend. I knew I should have called her to offer my condolences, but I had been too preoccupied with my own problems. Knowing her, she was probably keeping track of me from a distance. She must have known that I was in Washington because Mario had been very insistent that Ivan Rosenbluth represented me.

A uniformed guard came over and stood directly in front of me. Aware of what he was looking for, I ignored him hoping that he would go away, but he didn't.

"Do you have a badge, sir?" he asked pleasantly.

"I do," I said abrasively pulling it out of my pocket. "I don't want to advertise who I am. There are a lot of crackpots here."

"There is nothing to fear Mr ... uh, Mr. Swager," he said reading the badge. "We are equipped to deal with any situation. I must insist that you wear it, in plain view."

"You can insist all you like, but I'll keep it in my pocket anyway. However, you could order me to leave, and I'd gladly oblige."

"Then why did you bother coming?"

"Ask Senator McBain; he invited me."

"I see by your ID that you are here to appear as a witness; you can't leave."

He raised his eyebrows and didn't say anymore but stepped back and spoke on his radio, to return a moment later.

"It's quite all right, Mr. Swager. Everything is straightened out. I'm sorry for the misunderstanding. May I escort you to your seat?"

"No thanks, I know where it is."

He stood beside me rocking back and forth from his toes to his heels. He didn't seem to notice my unpleasant attitude. He was probably used to people snapping at him; the realization of this made me apologize for my bad manners.

Ivan Rosenbluth was a well-known lawyer in Buffalo. He was tall and lean, with over-sized flat-feet pointing outwards. People often referred to him as Kermit. Client privilege meant nothing to the Mafia lawyer. He would report everything to his boss. He looked very impressive rummaging through his papers, but he would be of little use. Finally standing up, Kermit looked at his watch then looked around the room. When he spotted me, he sat down. Almost instantly, he got up again and looked past me towards the door. Curious I also turned to look. Amelia was standing in the doorway. She saw me as soon as I stepped away from the wall and came right over and kissed my cheek. Taking a tissue from her purse, she wiped the lipstick from my face. Her deep brown eyes were teasing. She didn't hold any grudges.

"Do you mind that I came?"

"No ... I'm surprised but glad. You're probably the only friend here, except for my bodyguard."

"What about Ivan?" she asked teasingly. She knew how I felt about him. "He's on your side."

"Yeah, he's on my side but not as a friend. You know how I feel about lawyers. Kermit is especially slippery. Mario probably sent him to make sure that I don't sell him down the tubes ... Damn it's good to see you."

"I take it you missed me?"

"Well ... yeah, I just don't want to send you a wrong signal."

"Hey, you missed me, that's good enough for me."

"Won't give up will you, Amelia?"

"Nope, but we'll talk about that later Mickey."

"Where are you staying?"

"With you of course."

"Like hell."

"Oh, come on, Mickey, don't be so difficult. You know that you want me to, you're just playing hard-to-get."

I tried to be stronger than the last time I'd been with her, but it was no use. She had already rekindled the fire. It was obvious that she meant every word she'd said in Buffalo. She wouldn't give up. Our relationship had changed drastically since that first night. She wasn't just beautiful, she was smart and knew exactly what she wanted. Perhaps I should smarten up and marry her and divorce my ghost.

I took my place at the table beside Ivan who had been waiting impatiently.

"What the hell is she doing here?"

"Hey it's a free country, ain't it?"

"For Christ sake, Swager, don't you think that they know who she is?"

"Maybe ... I don't know, but they sure as hell will before this is over. She doesn't take orders from you or me. You know something Ivan, you're too uptight. Why don't you go for a nice long swim tonight? It's a natural thing to do, you'll feel better."

"Fuck you, Swager! I don't like you any more than you do me."

"Then why not get your ass out of here, I sure as hell don't need you."

"I'm here to look after your interests, whether you believe it or not."

"Uh uh, you're here because Mario told you to be."

"Whatever! Don't answer anything without clearing it with me first."

"Hey, I'm not one of Mario's employees. Besides I'm protected by the immunity clause in the agreement."

He shrugged as if he didn't care, but the publicity was important to him.

The teenager stared at me. She watched my every move, and this bothered me. What was she doing there anyway? She should have been in school.

The proceedings were supposed to start at ten sharp. At twenty past ten, my patience was running out, and at ten-thirty I made up my mind that it was time for a coffee break. I got up and was about to leave when the committee members came in. The three-member panel sat down on the podium and the chairman started by introducing himself as James McBain. I knew what he looked like because I had seen his picture while I was doing my research.

He was a heavyset man of average height and balding. A fact he tried to camouflage it by styling his thinning red hair in a major "comb-over." He was an ugly man with or without hair. His pudgy pink, pockmarked face looked worse in person. He introduced Mr. Jack Balinsky to his right and Mr. Timothy Anderson to his left, filled a glass of water and began.

"We are pleased that you were able to attend these proceedings, Mr. Swager. Please, place your left hand on the Bible, raise your right hand and repeat after me."

"What for?"

"To be sworn in."

"Again, what for?"

"Let's not be difficult about this, Mr. Swager."

"I am not being difficult, sir, and I do not believe being sworn in is necessary. You have asked me to come to answer questions for which you have no answers. I came, to tell the truth. If not, I would have stayed home. Ask your questions and let's not play political or moral games."

"Very well, Mr. Swager. I can see that you aren't going to be a very co-operative witness. Will you please state your name and address?"

"My name is Michael Avery Swager. I am a citizen of Canada."

"We would like to have your exact address as well."

"I am sure you would if you didn't already have it. Publicizing it isn't in my best interest."

Shaking his head, he continued, "it has been brought to our attention that you carry a concealed weapon ... well, Mr. Swager?"

"Well, what? What is your question, sir?"

"Are you armed? Are you carrying a gun right now?"

"I am, and I do."

"In that case, I must ask you to hand it over to the security guard for safekeeping; it will be returned to you upon leaving the premises."

The guard, who Dan had given a hard time earlier, now stepped forward with a big grin on his face.

"No, Senator. It is already very safe, with me. Under no circumstance will I hand it over. You have been made aware of the terms of the agreement for me to appear before this committee. However, since all or some of it may have slipped your mind, let me clear up a few things you do not or choose not to remember. The agreement is between myself and your department of justice, and it is endorsed by the US Attorney General.

Item 1: I am permitted to carry a concealed weapon anywhere in the United States of America during my stay for these proceedings, so long as entry is granted to the premises.

Item 2: I have a guarantee of safe conduct. I can leave at any time of my choosing and return to Canada without hindrance.

Item 3: Nothing I say during these proceedings can be used as evidence against me in a court of law, and I answer only those questions that I am willing to answer."

"Well, Mr. Swager, that is a whole lot of agreements, but here you are on my turf, and I can't have people with guns running around, so if you please."

"In that case Senator I will abide by the rules of your turf, but I'll also opt to enact Item 2: in the agreement and leave."

Getting up from my chair, I stepped away from the table and turned to leave.

"Now hold on, Mr. Swager, let's not be too hasty about this, let me have a moment to confer with my colleagues."

Kermit looked pained, holding his hand against his forehead. He could lose me before my testimony even started, which also meant losing days of media attention and his retainer.

McBain did as I expected. Killing me had failed, but he had to find out how much I knew about his connection to Geoffrey Savoy.

"Under the circumstances, we agree to let you stay, but we insist that you show caution and good judgment."

"I am so very grateful for your generosity, Senator. I doubt, however, that I can be credited with having good judgment. After all, I am here ..."

"So you are, sir. If you are innocent of any wrongdoing, there shouldn't be any need for the immunity. Justice is equal for all in this country, even foreign nationals."

"Justice you say? A hell of a concept, the lady, truly is blind. As long as the state and privileged of society have better access to legal representation than the rest of society, there is very little justice. It is easy for the judicial system to wash its hands claiming that the system is just and its laws must be followed. If the scales of justice were truly balanced, the population of your penal institutions would reflect a fairer cross-section of color and race. Perhaps then, people like myself, wouldn't have to seek protection from injustice."

"Mr. Swager, this inquiry is about international drug trafficking, not civil rights or our legal system."

"You opened the door, lecturing me on justice. You were a judge at one time, Senator. How secure do you think I feel answering the questions of a man who has gone down the ladder from judge to a politician on a witch-hunt?"

"I resent that statement, but I can understand your feelings of hostility, Mr. Swager. The system isn't perfect, but it is all we have. You could always apply for citizenship and vote to change it."

"No thanks."

"I see that I have underestimated you. Your provocative skills tend to lead us away from the subject at hand."

"That's easily avoided by not telling me your problems, Senator."

"I will keep that in mind, sir."

He cleared his throat and drank some water. As a politician, he was better equipped with skills to draw me into his arena so, I had to be careful not to walk into a trap. Attacking his country and its laws could make me more enemies than allies.

"Mr. Swager, we have information that you have been instrumental in bringing a large quantity of contraband into the US. We believe that the shipment originated in Brazil. Since you cannot be held accountable for it with your immunity, you can admit to your involvement without fear of prosecution."

"I would be glad to confess, but your information is flawed, I can't help you."

"Cannot or will not, Mr. Swager? We realize that the information might implicate the people you work with but I can assure you, we will look after your safety at all times."

"Obviously I have my doubts about that or I wouldn't be carrying a gun. However, your information is wrong. I am a self-employed lumber broker, and I don't think that wood is considered an illegal substance."

"Then what is your association with the Galante family in Buffalo?"

"Well, Senator, most likely your information is gathered from gossip columns in the tabloids. I have never made a secret of dating Amelia Galante. Although her appearance may be intoxicating, I doubt that anyone can call her an illegal substance. However, I could have a problem with the Canadian Customs when I bring her home to meet my family. Her beauty could cause a riot in my family."

As angry as Mickey's answer made him, McBain had no choice but wait for the laughter to subside before he continued. I looked at Amelia. She was sitting a few yards away and not the least bit flustered. She smiled at a cameraman who was bold enough to come from the back of the room to capture her image. The guard promptly took his arm and escorted him away.

"A very entertaining speech during these otherwise dull proceedings, I must admit, Mr. Swager. The name Galante, however, is much more widely known than just in the streets of Buffalo. You must be aware of the family's reputation?"

"I'm not. I must plead ignorance. On the other hand, you display a high degree of arrogance, Senator, by assuming that the rest of the world cares what goes on in the streets of your cities. I, for one, pay very little attention to gossip, even less when it comes from political sources. If the Galante family is indeed a criminal organization, you should arrest them and put them in jail. Don't blame me for the criminal activities of your citizens. Don't come after me. "

"Were you not instrumental in bringing a shipment of cocaine into the US?"

"No sir."

"We have information from the DEA that links you directly to a smuggling operation."

"If that's the case, Senator, you should have another talk with your boys over at DEA. It is not unusual for them to regularly have problems with the English language confusing words such as information and disinformation."

"I thought that we agreed you would answer questions, Mr. Swager, but all you are doing is criticizing our government and its agencies. Your answers are beginning to sound like lectures."

"Ask me questions, and I will answer them to the best of my ability. I realize that an election is on the horizon Senator, but badgering me won't get you any votes."

"Were you not shot while visiting Buffalo, just last summer?"

Ah, a true question. "I was. Perhaps now, you can understand why I have my doubts about your ability to keep me safe."

"You can't blame that on an American, Mr. Swager. The police identified the assailant as a hired killer from Brazil."

"I'm sure glad about that. I'll sleep much better tonight. Too bad that this identification was not made before shooting me. He ran around this country with a gun, bigger than mine and no one ever asked him to hand it over for safe keeping."

"You seem to be determined to make me look bad."

"Not true, sir, it is quite evident that you don't need any of my help for that."

The Senator was fuming and continued questioning me for the entire day. I had a feeling that I had the upper hand over him as his patience wore thinner. He looked tired and old by the time he adjourned. I had spent the whole day trying to figure out what he really wanted from me. He made only one reference to Brazil which confirmed that he had me summoned for personal reasons. Had he asked me about Honduras, It could have meant he was legitimately interested in my involvement with drugs.

The teenager, who had shown an unusual interest in the hearings, was standing in the hall when we came out. Amelia gave me a tug when she saw me looking at her and said, "forget it, Mickey, she's much too young for you, besides she's the Senator's daughter."

Perhaps that was why she looked familiar. I must have seen her in one of the photographs. Looking back at her once more, our eyes met.

"Mickey ... knock it off, will you? I told you that she's too young. Quit while you're ahead or you sleep alone tonight."

"You don't have to threaten me; I am sleeping alone anyway. My room is much too dangerous for you. You saw how the Senator was ready to kill me, besides I need my rest."

"Now listen to me, I've come all this way to be with you, so unless you tell me there is something more going on than just looking between you and the kid, I'll be in your bed. As far as any danger is concerned, I can handle it."

She tapped her purse, and I knew what she meant. I left her standing in the hallway when a few reporters closed in on her. She didn't seem to mind the attention. Knowing her, she would probably expand on my earlier statement about our relationship. She broke loose when she saw that I had kept going and caught up with me right outside. The reporters gathered with trucks and cameras outside the building; it slowed me down. Microphones were shoved in my face along with more questions than I could possibly answer; my only reply was, "no comment." Once again, it was apparent that she enjoyed the attention. I, on the other hand, could have done without.

My original assessment of the hearings had obviously been wrong. If these were considered low key, I would have hated to be part of those rated high profile. The Senator's statement about Galante was right on the mark. I didn't know how infamous her family was but Amelia being with me was a bonus for the media. Some had us already engaged.

I watched as she hiked up her skirt and stepped into the van. Knowing that I would look, she winked at me. The cameras recorded her every move. Ben had trouble closing the doors, but he managed to whisk us away, much to the chagrin of the reporters left on the sidewalk. Their frenzy was understandable. My attitude and the fame of the Galante family fostered a great storyline. It's not unusual for the media to exploit the public's interest in the underworld by showing the romantic side of successful criminals. I was an unwilling participant. I was a victim of circumstances and would have preferred to stay out of the limelight.

The van was comfortably equipped with lounge chairs, tinted windows and a partition between the driver and passengers to give more privacy and security. Ben, who sat next to the driver, used the intercom to point out one more feature.

"There's an AK under the seat, just in case we run into a problem and need extra firepower."

I reached under his seat and found the assault rifle. I hated it, but I knew how Ben reasoned and should have expected a stunt like it. I didn't think that Ben had ever actually shot anyone, but he liked to picture himself as a macho soldier of fortune. I was unimpressed and unsure of the status of the weapon, which was most likely illegal. Ben's blatant disregard for the law could be costly.

"I want it gone, Ben, we both have guns. I can't run the risk of getting caught with it. I have immunity for things I say at the hearings, not laws I break while I'm here."

I took off my jacket and used it to wipe my fingerprints from the weapon, carefully putting it back under the seat. Amelia watched me and commented, "that wasn't smart, you can't wear that again until it's been cleaned, there is oil on it now. I'll send it down tonight."

"No rush. I have another suit. I won't be here long."

"You sure surprised me with that statement. It blew me away."

"Which one?"

"About taking me to meet your family."

"Don't take it seriously. It was meant as a diversion."

"So you actually don't care about me."

"No, I do care, and I do think that you are beautiful. But it must be obvious to you that there is more to me than being a mule for your old man."

"I know that Mickey, but when I saw you this morning I realized how much I missed you and I'm willing to do anything just to stay with you."

"Let's not get into that right now. I have too many other problems on my mind."

"It sounds as if you have thought about it too."

"Well ... actually, I have but not now, please."

She had a smile that told me she was hopeful and she would have continued to discuss the subject if I hadn't ended it by kissing her.

The driver took some extra detours to make sure that no overzealous reporters followed us to the hotel. We drove straight into the garage and entered the service elevator. At the room, Ben went in ahead and gave the room a quick inspection.

"I still think it was a dumb idea to come here. You should have stayed home and let them come to you."

"Yeah ... maybe, you saw how well that went, besides I have to get this over with and get on with my life. You saw what they tried to do to me at home. If I hadn't come here, it would go on until they succeeded. I don't want to be constantly looking over my shoulder. Maybe this will put a stop to it."

"You know something Mick; it might be a good idea for me to bunk in with you."

"No thanks. There's only one bed."

"They can send up a cot, or I can sleep on the couch."

"I'm not in that much danger and two is a company, but three is a crowd."

"She's staying with you?"

"Yeah, I guess. "She," might not like having you around tonight."

"She" had been listening to our conversation and wanted to know more.

"What happened at home, Mickey?"

"Oh, it was really no big deal."

"Not a big deal," mouthed Ben. "If you'd opened that friggin, door you would've been hamburger for Christ sake."

"Is there anything I can do about it, Mickey?"

"Like hell! How can I get it through to you that you're not my guardian angel? The Galante family has done me enough favors. Look how Mario took care of the guy in Buffalo. No thanks."

It was Ben's turn to be surprised.

"That Senator wasn't lying, was he? You didn't tell me anything about problems in Buffalo. You expect me to look after your safety, but you don't think that it is necessary to tell me these things."

"If you don't like it, you can leave," snapped Amelia. "I can handle the job just fine. I am better at it than you … big shot! I can watch him twentyfour hours a day."

"Look, I don't need you, or anyone else, hassling me right now."

Ben left for his room.

I went over to the bar to get a drink to calm my nerves. I was beginning to have second thoughts about staying to testify but leaving could make matters worse. I had no sooner opened the ice bucket when she said, "no Mickey, I'll do that."

Watching her as she stood at the bar, I felt badly for snapping at her. I knew how sensitive she was. I walked up behind her and put my arms around her. I looked at her in the mirror. She was beautiful even when she cried. Bowing her head, she tried to hide her tears because she knew how uncomfortable it made me.

"I'm sorry, Amie, I shouldn't have spoken to you like that. I didn't mean to hurt you, I'm sorry."

"I know you are. I know what you are going through."

"I doubt it."

It was time to change the subject.

"I missed you a lot after I left Buffalo."

"You could have called me; I would have come."

"Yeah, I know. That's what is so troublesome. I know you love me unconditionally. I also know that I love you but with reservations. I can't run the risk of making us both unhappy. You might be interested to know, I made up my mind before leaving home. I'm going to find Maggie and get things settled once and for all."

Her tears were gone, and my drink was forgotten. Her eyes filled with fire when she pulled away from me.

"That scares the crap out of me. I could lose you forever. I might not be able to compete with her. I would rather have part of you than nothing at all. What I have now is a sure thing. She might take that away from me if you see her again. Marry me! That will be enough for me."

"Can't do that. I promised the Mongoose that I would only marry you if I knew that it would be forever."

"You discussed this with him? You didn't tell me. Why would you go to him with something that was so private?"

"I didn't. He came to Montreal before he died. He wanted me to marry you."

"That SON-OF-A-BITCH!" she barked. "He probably offered you money."

"Ah … well … I …"

"How much?" she asked as her lips became harsh, forming a thin line.

"How much? Ah … two … two million."

"The bastard!" she yelled, banging her fist on the dresser.

"Hey, … you know how he was, Amelia."

"Why are you telling me this now?" she demanded angrily as she spun around and stared at me. "Do you want to rub my nose in it, is that it?"

"Come on, Amelia, I want things to be open and above board between us. I didn't want it to be a surprise later on."

"I would very much like you to come clean with me, Mickey. I'll tell you what, I'll write you a check for the two right now, and you can walk away, no questions asked. You don't have to marry me. I'll give you the money, no strings attached."

"Do you really feel it necessary to test me? Do you think that I'd be tempted? If you are that unsure or if there's anything that makes you believe I haven't been honest with you, you should go now. I don't want you here if you don't trust me. I didn't go to your father; he came to me."

She was silent and stared at the floor as she drew lines in the pile of the carpet with the heel of her shoe. "I … I don't know what to say. I don't want to go. I know how I feel about you. I have already said that I'll take you no matter what and I mean it."

Probably realizing that her proposal was as insane and

insulting as her father's, she added, "I trust you, Mickey. I was being mean, and I'm sorry."

"Amelia … Look, look at me. I'll tell you what I told your old man. Neither the family, the business, nor the two million make any difference. I'll ask you to marry me when nothing stands in the way."

"You told him that? Even Mario never talked to him like that. I … I … I'm sorry, Mickey, I didn't mean to be like him but when you talk about going to find her … well … it scares me to death."

"Please try to understand, Amie. There are so many things that I love about you, but there are also so many memories of her. Maybe they are unrealistic, but I have to find out for sure. I was 21 when she left me. Many things have happened since.

"So, you're not telling me that it's over between us?"

"Well, actually, I have to admit that I have probably fallen in love with you but I have to get the other stuff out of the way before I can even think about asking you to marry me. I'm not sure if it was a good idea to admit this, but I owe you that much."

"You know something … I'm not so scared anymore. I'm going to fight like hell."

"I hope that you would just do me one favor, leave your gun out of it."

13

The night was warm and the endless wailing sirens of ambulances, police cars and other emergency vehicles, kept me awake. I sat in the dark trying to get my thoughts together when I noticed someone's shadow through the crack under my door. I looked for my gun but remembered putting it in the closet. I didn't want to waken Amelia, so I looked for hers in her purse. It wasn't there. Although I had a preference for baseball bats, I grabbed a heavy glass ashtray from the desk and waited near the door. I expected to see the doorknob turn. Instead, a piece of paper was slipped under the door. I waited for the mysterious messenger to leave before picking it up. I was about to turn the light on in the bathroom when I looked towards the bed. Amelia was sitting up holding her gun.

"Jesus! ... get that piece out of my face, Amelia."

"Next time keep yours under your pillow like I do mine, and this won't happen." She said in a sleepy voice.

She put the gun back, flopping down she started to laugh.

"This isn't a laughing matter. You're barely awake. You could have shot me for Christ sake."

Don't worry I'm awake enough. I was just laughing because you piddled your pants."

I immediately looked down.

"Gotcha," she laughed.

I read the note; it was from Mario. It was some dirt on Jack Balinsky. I flushed it down the toilet and went back to bed. Amelia was still snickering, "did you?" "Did I what?"

"Piss your pants."

I was up early and a good thing too, I'd forgotten how much time a woman needs in the bathroom. I thought about Mario's note. I had to trust that the information had been double-checked. He wouldn't deliberately hang me out to dry. Not because he was looking out for my best interests but because more importantly to damage the committee image. Balinsky was on the same team as McBain, and this was war. Reason enough to take a swing at him.

Ben had managed to get clearance to park the van in the lot behind the building, so we could come and go via the back door to avoid the press. When we came down the long hall, a fart echoed from an office. Amelia started to laugh with a loud snort. Senator McBain stuck his head out of the doorway when he heard her. His pudgy face turned purple, and he ducked back inside when we passed his office. Amelia looked in through the open door. He was putting his jacket on, and she said, "that one must have come from Chicago, Senator."

"I beg your pardon ma'am?" He looked puzzled, "Chicago ...?"

"Yeah, the Windy City."

He looked at the label inside his jacket. "No, it's from New York?"

"No sir, I meant your windbreaker."

He obviously lacked a sense of humor and slammed the door shut without answering her which led her to bury her face in her hand and let out another snort. She didn't stop laughing until we came to the entrance. The press was waiting. Not shy, she walked freely amongst the reporters and camera crews. Perhaps it wasn't smart to have her with me during the messy affair, but it was too late to change anything. Besides, it gave my statement about our dating, credibility. The young girl was back. She came over and gave me an envelope. The guard tried to stop her, but I dismissed him with a polite thank you and took the envelope. There was no name on it, but there was a note not to open it until I was alone. I looked at her and put it in my inside pocket. She left the room, and I didn't see her for the rest of the day. Kermit had seen her and asked if there was anything he should be looking at. Still standing I shook my head without answering.

"It could be a message from McBain, I think that I should look at it," he insisted.

Although the envelope was burning a hole in my pocket, I respected her wish to wait until later.

"No Ivan, I already know what's in it. She's a teenager with a crush on me."

Kermit leaned forward almost salivating, "I'll give it to her if you're not interested."

Appearing to ignore his remark, I lifted my chair closer to the table and flopped down. One of the chair legs landed on Kermit's foot, and he started cursing and swearing while grabbing his foot. I feigned total innocence.

"Oh my God, Ivan ... I'm so sorry! I didn't realize that your foot was there. Is there anything I can do? I hope it's not broken. I'm so sorry."

He didn't answer but gave me a painful stare that told me he didn't believe one word.

He limped away from his seat, probably to find someplace to check the damage to his foot.

Amelia had seen the commotion and came to investigate.

"What's with Ivan?" she whispered in my ear.

"His foot ... I accidentally put my chair on it."

"Is he okay?"

"Yeah ... he will be when the pain goes away, but he'll be swimming in circles from now on."

"I can see on your face that you did it on purpose Mickey. You're not that clumsy."

"Well ... no, it wasn't an accident, but it serves him right, I didn't like what that pig said about the McBain girl."

"Oh, I see ... he started that crap with me once."

"Don't worry Amie, if he tries it again, I'll fix his other foot, and he'll swim straight again."

Kermit limped back in time for McBain to call the proceedings to order.

He kept hammering at my connections with the Mafia. It didn't bother me one bit because it's not a crime but the fact that he didn't talk about Brazil anymore was beginning to bother me. Maybe he was trying another tactic. I had seen Balinsky get impatient. I wanted him to get involved so I could knock him out of the game by using Mario's information. It wasn't until the afternoon that Balinsky asked his first question.

"Is it true, Mr. Swager, that you plan to marry Miss Galante, the daughter of the gangster, known as the Mongoose?"

I didn't expect him to be that blunt.

"First of all, it is none of your business what my plans are. You're just being nosy. Secondly, Sir! I don't like to have the people with whom I associate, referred to as gangsters. Mr. Alphonse Galante passed away six weeks ago. You insulted the man's memory with your unfounded innuendo, and I demand an apology!"

"The fact that the man is dead doesn't change anything, Mr. Swager, the criminal activities will be carried on by his successor, as sure as the sun rises each day."

"How dare you speak ill of others. You are one of the most dishonest people in this room and yet, there you sit, in judgment of others."

"What in the world are you talking about, Mr. Swager? This isn't about me; it is about you."

"Uh uh, it isn't just about me. The three of you are very much a part of this. You have investigated me for a long time and haven't been able to find anything illegal about me or my business. If you had, you would have indicted me and had me extradited under the agreements between our respective countries. In spite of your lack of information, I have come here of my own free will. Not, however, before I launched an investigation of my own and found you, Mr. Balinsky, to be particularly unsuitable to be questioning me about my conduct."

"Well Mr. Swager I don't care a whole lot whether you find me suitable or not; you're stuck with me."

"Not when the press prints what I have to say. You'll be running for cover, instead of office."

"So you found out I took a pencil home from the office six months ago, did you? or ...?"

I unceremoniously interrupted his nonsense:

"Mr. Balinsky, my grandfather told me a long time ago, to never trust a man who cheats on his wife, because he won't hesitate to cheat anyone else either."

McBain was taking a keen interest in the exchange. Getting me angry was just what he wanted because an angry man makes mistakes.

Balinsky shifted in his chair. It creaked loudly in the now silent room, and then he practically shouted, "just go with me on this, Swager, and stick to the matter at hand. Your grandfather's advice is of very little use to you during these proceedings."

"I am very well aware of that, sir, but I will not have my morals questioned by a man who cheats on his wife."

Balinsky reddened, shuffled some papers on his desk and fiddled with his water-glass, obviously, stalling for time. Calm and self-assured, I liked my place in the driver's seat. The room was silent. Attacking an opponent with words was far more enjoyable than with a baseball bat. The adrenaline was flowing as the tables were turning. I was on the attack. McBain saw it happening, but he didn't interfere. I kept up the momentum.

"You have a mistress. Her name is Marilyn Ashton. You keep her in an apartment and pay her rent."

Balinsky stood up and banged his fist on the table. "That's a lie! I'll have you in court, I'll sue you for slander!" he shouted.

"Be my guest. You'll never win because it is true. By the way, she isn't very faithful. She has other clients. I could go on and advertise her address, but I think that you get my drift and you know how reporters are. They'll get all the juicy details."

Balinsky turned ashen, stood up and left the room.

McBain seemed to want to speak. I felt he might try to lessen the impact of the moment by changing the subject, But I wanted to use the opportunity to my best advantage.

McBain finally said, "under the circumstances, I think an adjournment is ..."

It was my turn to pound a fist on the table.

"No! ... no sir ... excuse me, Senator! I have not quite finished. I demand an apology, or I will not be back here until I get it."

McBain didn't hesitate. He had the unpleasant task of apologizing and was visibly furious over the incident. I had shown him that I could play dirty and I felt a rush having dealt them a crushing blow.

"You are right of course, I am sorry, the behavior of my colleague was inexcusable, and the buck stops here. My apologies to you sir, and to the bereaved family of the late Mr. Galante … These proceedings are adjourned until Monday morning."

The Senator got up and left without waiting for Anderson. The media pushed and shoved, vying for a better position, even though they knew that I wouldn't give them anything based on the day before, but they had to try. We slowly made our way into the hall, where it had become impossible to move. I looked around to see if there was any other way out. The only alternative was to go back into the room and wait for things to quieten down. I turned and came face to face with Amelia. She wasn't the least bit flustered but giggled, "the Senator's wind-breaker would clear this place in a hurry."

I couldn't help but laugh and dismissed a tap on my shoulder as another reporter trying to get my attention. Whoever it was, was persistent and I turned to look. It was the security guard who smiled and motioned me to follow. Hoping that he didn't hold a grudge, we went back into the room we had just fought to leave. We stayed close behind him as he took us to the front of the hall and out through the door used by the committee members. It led to a narrow, windowless hallway that ran behind the chambers. Halfway down, we were stopped by the fat Senator, planted squarely in the middle, with his hands on his hips. There was no room to pass.

"This is off limits to the public, you have to go back."

Squeezing past the guard who was ready to obey orders, I looked straight at McBain.

"Senator, I don't know what you have against me but whatever it is, is probably personal. We could have worked things out privately but for some reason, you dragged me into this, and I will damn well find out what's bugging you before I leave. We're just using this exit to get away from the media. You must know that talking to the press won't do either one of us any good."

"I have no idea what you are talking about, Swager. I have nothing against you. All I want is the truth about your involvement in the drug trade."

"Senator, my only involvement with drugs is Aspirin for my headaches and Preparation H for my dealings with you. You have become a real pain in the ass."

"You are speaking to a United States Senator, not some junky in the gutter. I am entitled to some respect."

"Then earn it before you demand it! What I have learned about you may also be of great interest to the press. They'll have a ball speculating about your reasons for having me come to Washington. It will become clear that I have nothing to do with drugs, and that this is all part of your own agenda. I don't have all the pieces of the puzzle yet, but I'll sure have them before I leave this neck of the woods, and so will everyone else."

"I will let you pass here this time, not because I'm intimidated by your bizarre speculations but because I'm getting tired of your belligerence. In the future, you will have to leave like everyone else via the main exits."

He went back into his chambers and slammed the door.

"What the hell was all that about, Mickey?"

"It's something between him and me."

"You knew him before you came here?"

"No, I knew of him."

She sensed that I wasn't about to give any more information, so she didn't ask. Back in the room, I took my jacket and holster off and threw them on the bed. The victory of the day was mine. I'd won a skirmish. The war could wait until the following week. I tried to imagine what Balinsky would go through by the time he got home ... or to his mistress. A victory drink was in order.

Amelia took the jacket and hung it in the closet. She noticed the envelope sticking out of the pocket.

"Here, Mickey, the letter from your young admirer."

I had completely forgotten about it but opened it immediately.

Dear Mr. Swager:

I am sorry that my father has taken it upon himself to persecute you. He is not a bad person even though he can be difficult. He has been good to mom and me. He is only trying to do the right thing, and I doubt if he means to harm you. A deep rift has developed between my parents over this, with my mother taking your side and not supporting my dad's position. There has never been much affection between them but these last months things have worsened. I don't know what caused all this. I have asked him, but he will not tell me. I love both my parents. Although I have never been close to my dad, I know that he loves me. Mom and I have always had a very close relationship, but she also keeps silent. Perhaps you can shed some light on this mystery. There are many things I wish to ask you. I can't believe that you are as bad as my dad makes you out to be especially since my mom seems to believe you are kind and considerate of others. That is why I am asking for a chance to talk to you.

Yours truly: Belinda McBain

She sounded sincere. I had never given McBain's family any thought. The girl must have been confident that I wouldn't publish the letter. I should meet with her and find out what she wanted. She was very young and probably never thought of the implications of putting in writing anything that could harm her father. Perhaps she was melodramatic, one of those things kids do, to call attention to themselves. I had no experience with teenagers, but I would have to give her the benefit of the doubt. She hadn't given me her phone number. Maybe she didn't want her parents to know that she had contacted me.

I sat down and sipped my drink while watching Amelia tidying the room. My eyelids were getting heavy, and I put the glass on the table …

"Come on Mickey, wake up."

She stroked my hair and kissed me. I looked into her eyes and felt comfortable and relaxed. Her love for me was impossible to ignore, and it cast a spell that threatened my commitment to finding Maggie. I couldn't let that happen, but I couldn't hurt Amelia. She certainly had compounded my problems by showing up.

"Come on Mickey, I like it when you hold me but relax, you're holding me too tight. It hurts when you do that."

I let her go when the phone rang.

"I am sorry to disturb you Mr. Swager; it's Belinda McBain. I was wondering if you have read my letter."

"Yeah, I did. I don't know how I can help you, but I am willing to talk to you. How about tomorrow, the hearings are suspended until Monday anyway."

"No ... no ... tomorrow is no good; I will be at the hospital most of the day."

"I'm sorry, nothing serious I hope?"

"No, I ... I'm on dialysis."

"I am sorry to hear that, maybe I could come to the hospital to talk."

"Oh, yeah that would be neat, it will make the time go faster, it's so boring."

She gave me directions.

"Okay, I will see you tomorrow."

Belinda looked small sitting in the big recliner. Her bright, blue eyes had a sadness about them. She studied me as I sat facing her. We sat in silence while I admired her youthful face. Neither sadness nor illness touched her natural beauty. Seeing her become uncomfortable with either my silence or the fact that I was staring at her prompted me to start talking.

"I'm sorry that you aren't well. I hope you will get better soon."

"No, it doesn't look like it. I need a new kidney. Maybe some accident victim will show up in the register and match."

"Is there no chance for a transplant any other way?"

"No, they only do it with a close relative, like a brother

or sister. They checked mom and dad, but they don't match, and I am an only child."

"Maybe in time, you will get better."

"No ... they're shot, they're shot to hell, even the dialysis is not working well anymore. Strange, I'm waiting for somebody to die so that I can live."

She tried to give the impression that she accepted things the way they were. She had a carefree look on her face, but I saw through her attempt to be brave. The chances of finding a suitable donor were slim. I listened as she talked about her life with her parents. They had never gotten along with each other. She admitted that her sympathies were with her mother. They were very close, and she spoke more of her as a friend or an older sister. Her father had always been too busy to pay any attention to her. She finally asked him her first question.

"Why is my dad angry with you?"

"I don't know. I don't know him or anyone else in Washington for that matter. I was hoping that you could tell me a few things to help clear things up."

"I don't know. It started a couple of years ago before I became ill. Mom and dad had another huge fight, and she became quiet after that. She has always been sort of a sad person, but after that day she became really withdrawn."

"Maybe, because you were sick."

"No, I got sick after the big bust. Mom just became more withdrawn, and dad just stayed away from home as much as possible."

"I don't know, Belinda. I have tried everything to keep out of his way, ever since he first asked me to come here."

"Why, if you don't know what he wants."

"No, you don't understand. I don't know what he has against me, but I think I know what he wants."

"What, what does he want?"

"It's best if I wait to tell you after the hearings."

They continued to talk. Belinda worried about what her mother would do after she had died. She had no family or close friends. All the people she did know were dad's political cronies.

When I left, it occurred to me that neither of us was any the wiser. If anything, I was probably more confused. Maybe McBain would back off after seeing the way I had hammered Balinsky at the inquiry. The only proof I had about the involvement of McBain in the attempt on my life was Savoy's confession. Although I had no hard evidence, a thorough investigation could substantiate the accusations. The fact that McBain was chairman of this committee was too much of a coincidence. The whole mess was going to ruin his family and his career if he persisted unless of course, he succeeded in getting me killed.

14

"What do you want me to wear for dinner tonight, Mickey?"

"I don't know, ask me about what you should wear to bed, and I'll tell you."

"You have a one-track mind."

"Hey, you're the one that kept me from going blind."

"What the heck do you mean?"

"Never mind, it's a long story.

Although it was a pleasure having her around, I had to get used to the bathroom being used mostly by her. It wasn't just a bathroom anymore but also a laundry and dressing room. There was never any shampoo nor clean towels, and pantyhose hanging over the shower rod.

"You are taking me out for dinner tonight, aren't you?"

"Yeah ... but I want to go early before it gets too busy."

"Ben isn't coming too, is he?"

"He is, but he won't be sitting with us. He said that he is concerned after the Balinsky thing. He wants to keep an eye on things from a distance. I think that he's exaggerating, but did I hire him to watch my butt.

"Thank God. I can't stand him. He behaves as if every woman is a whore."

"Yeah I know, he doesn't want people to think that he might like boys better."

She stepped out from the bathroom holding her ponytail with one hand and taking a hairpin out of her mouth with the other. Amused as well as surprised she said, "for real, he's one of those guys?"

"I'm not sure, but any guy who always talks about women the way he does has problems. He probably feels inadequate as a man and just as probably, making tough, derogatory remarks makes him feel like the man he wants to be."

"You don't mind homosexuals?"

"No, why?"

"Most guys can't stand them."

"That's their problem. I believe that all people have a right to be happy no matter what. As long as gay people don't mind me being straight, there isn't a problem."

"You really do feel that way, don't you?"

"I do now, but I used to be as prejudiced as every other red-blooded redneck."

"What made you change?"

"Time ... maybe I grew up, who knows."

The hotel dining room was busy. Mickey had almost finished his drink, and they had decided what they wanted to order. He looked around for someone to serve them. A young man came sauntering over to their table with his raincoat carelessly hanging open and a baseball cap pulled low over his eyes. It made me suspicious.

"You Mickey Swager?"

"Yeah, I'm Mickey Swager, what can I do for you?"

Unlike me, Ben handled the situation correctly and the guy was on the floor before he could answer. He was on top of him holding his head down against the floor, while he tried to force a sawed-off shotgun out of his hand. Amelia's face had turned to stone, her eyes harsh and sharp with the muzzle of her gun in his ear she said, "let go of that piece, or your brain is potato salad."

He dropped his shotgun, and Amelia waited until Ben had him hand-cuffed before she put the gun back in her purse. I could empathize with the prisoner as he was yanked to his feet by the handcuffs. But I still couldn't suppress his grin.

Ben stood around for a moment as if he expected a pat on the back for a job well done. When nothing happened, he looked at Amelia and smiled, "Thanks, honey, you're fast with that thing."

Her tone said it all, "call me honey again and this sucker will be in your ear."

"Wow! Sorry ... I didn't know you were so sensitive."

"Don't ever call me that again! I don't like you or your arrogant, chauvinistic attitude. This guy should never have gotten this far. He was very obvious, wearing a raincoat on a day like today. You should have stopped him at the door."

"Hey, I got him. Didn't I?"

"Yeah, you got him; next time 'got him' sooner. While

we are still on speaking terms, get Mickey a vest … today! I have watched your bungling from the get-go. If Mickey dies, you won't have to worry about me. My brother is less patient or forgiving than I."

"Knock it off, Amelia, he doesn't work for you, besides it's my ass on the line.

"Ben marched the would-be assassin towards the door as Amelia mumbled loud enough for me to hear.

"Yeah … you and me both; I won't put up with much more of his crap. Your being dead doesn't hurt you, but it does me."

Amelia closed her purse putting it beside her. It took her a moment to get rid of the anger in her eyes.

"You've got to be more careful, Mickey. That shit almost whacked you, and there you sit calmly as a cucumber. You don't seem to care; you act as if nothing has happened. God … you can be so frustrating! Where is your gun anyway?"

"Upstairs."

"A lot of good it does up there when you're being shot at down here."

"Yes ma'am, although yours here, is dangerous enough."

"What's that supposed to mean?"

"I know about the hair-trigger on that thing."

"So?"

"Having it in your lap right across from me could make me a *tenor* or worse. Why the hell did you cock it?"

"It's faster and more accurate."

"Yeah … like hell … To you, it could have been goodbye

marriage and kids, to me ... no more standing in the boy's room."

"Don't joke, Mickey; you don't seem to realize how serious the situation is."

"I do, but I can't become paranoid. I've been living with a price on my head for a long time."

"Yes I know about Rojas, and you told me about this guy in Montreal."

"Yeah ... well, they weren't the only ones. There was a guy in Brazil he had a contract on me."

"So that's why you left in a hurry ... do you know why?"

"No, not why, just who."

"Who?"

"McBain."

"WHAT?"

"McBain ... James McBain."

"For Christ sake! You know, and you came here anyway. You're giving him the perfect opportunity to finish the job."

"I know, but I didn't have much choice. I don't know why he wants me dead and I thought that by coming here I could find out."

"Aren't you here to testify about drugs?"

"Naah ... officially, yes, but that's just a smokescreen. He wants me on a slab in the morgue."

"That's it, Danny, from now on I'll sit with you and Ivan ... Does Ivan know about this?"

"No, he and Mario both think that it's about drugs. You know that he wouldn't have sent Ivan here just for me.

"You should have told me about this. I could have gotten

some more information about him. You say that you don't know him, but there must be something he knows about you."

"Yeah … I gathered as much a long time ago."

"What happened to the guy in Brazil?"

"Took care of him."

"Like Louie?"

"Yeah … like Louie."

"I have a big stake in you, Mickey. I meant what I said; I don't have any reason to live, with you dead. I think that we should go up and order room service."

"Naah … I came to eat, and that's what I'm going to do."

"Damn, you can be so pig-headed!"

"Yeah … I've been told that before. By the way, what did you mean when you said: "you and me both"?

"When?"

"When I asked you to take it easy on Ben."

"Oh, that … nothing."

"Come on, Amelia. You never say anything without reason."

"Well it was a slip of the tongue, but since you picked up on it, I might as well tell you. He's getting a bonus if he does the job well."

"You went behind my back?"

"No, I didn't. I did something without telling you, as you have done to me. Remember the two million, Mickey?"

"Yeah, I guess I had that coming. If we get ever get married, we'll have to get that crap out of the way and trust each other a little more … You don't like Ben; why pay him a bonus?"

"I had to, Mickey, you would spot one of Mario's men too easily."

She took a tissue out of her purse and checked her eye makeup in the mirror of her compact.

"You crying again?"

"No, I'm not! Just an eyelash. I just like what you say sometimes."

"Things ... like what?"

"Like hearing you talk about us getting married. I just wish that you would be more direct about it and not make it sound like ..."

"Like what?"

"Well like ... oh never mind. It is almost as if you have made up your mind to marry me, and you expect me just to take it ..."

"You're probably right; it's just ... well, I guess you've kind of grown on me. Having you with me feels so comfortable."

"WHAT ... comfortable! You talk about me as if I'm an old sock or a comfortable pair of slippers. GOD, you can be so ... so ... urf!

"Hey, I'm sorry. I've been living alone for so long, I just don't know how to do that romantic stuff. I didn't think I that could ever feel this way. I mean, I've been reconsidering my plans about looking for Maggie, but I don't know how to talk to you about stuff like that because you get carried away."

She suddenly lit up; dinner, guns, and Ben forgotten, the smile on her face lit up the entire room.

"I can't believe what I'm hearing, Mickey. I have thought about nothing else."

"Yeah ... well, let's not get ahead of ourselves. I'm not out of the woods yet. I wouldn't want you to be a grieving widow. I guess that my planned tour of the city and the trip to Arlington tomorrow is out."

"Damn right, Danny, I don't much care for your story of the widow."

Ben brought Dan the bulletproof vest right after dinner, and I tried it on. I looked in the mirror and saw that I had gained thirty pounds instantaneously. Ben must have sensed that something was wrong because he asked a bit sheepishly.

"Something wrong, Mick ... besides me screwing-up?"

"Well ... yeah ... I've got to let you go."

"Why, because I screwed-up?"

"No, because I can't trust you."

"Can't trust me; what the Christ is this about?"

"Taking money for my protection behind my back is a bad sign. It makes me wonder about your obligation to me is secondary to your greed. I should have trusted my first intuition when you got pissed-off about my comment the night I hired you."

"What the hell are you going to do for Christ sake; they're shooting real bullets at you man. Are you going to rely on that skirt to protect you?"

"That skirt's only interest is my safety; yours is money. Your check will be in the mail the day I get home. Refer to her again as a skirt when I'm around, and you'll find out that I have other skills besides inspecting lumber."

Seeing his anger as he walked away I realized that my

old friend who had become an acquaintance and was now a stranger, one step away from being an enemy.

"I've got a feeling that you didn't lose no … sorry, I have a feeling that you didn't lose a friend, Mickey; he was more like a leech."

"Well … yeah, you could be right, we lost our friendship a long time ago. It is just hard to think of him as an enemy.

It was late Saturday afternoon. After putting my gun on the desk and hanging the vest over a chair, I stood in front of the window, leafing quietly through a magazine. Amelia was rinsing something out in the bathroom. My silence caught her attention, and she peeked around the corner. Startling me by yelling in Buffalonian, "damn it, Mickey! Get away from the friggin windaw! You make a pufect target."

Too late. A shot rang out, knocking me to the floor. I tried to get up.

"Mickey! Stay down and make like you're dead or the son-of-a-bitch will take another crack at you!"

I stayed down and watched her crawl along the floor; gun firmly clenched in her hand. When she reached the window, she peered over the sill.

"Must be long gone by now," she mumbled turning towards me

I felt a strange detachment as I felt the warm blood running down the side of my face and saw the crimson drops falling on the carpet. The shot to my head made me think about Savoy … I tried to feel for an exit wound, but there wasn't one. I touched the wound expecting to find a hole there, but there was only a burning pain and blood. With Amelia's help, I pulled myself up on the bed.

"Take it easy Mickey, keep your fingers away from the wound, you don't want an infection."

"It's okay, honey, the bullet didn't go in, it only grazed me."

I expected coming to Washington would be dangerous and I had been far too reckless. It had taken being shot a second time for reality to sink in. Amelia brought a towel and checked the wound confirming what I already knew; it was only superficial. She went with me in the ambulance and held my hand. She had that soft, mushy look in her eyes.

"See Amelia, a lot of good that stupid vest was. Get your money back and buy me a helmet. Whoever wants to get me, wants to make sure by putting a slug in my brain."

"It's nothing to joke about, Mickey. If you would only learn to listen to me, you'd be a lot better off."

"Not necessarily. I'd be married."

"Alright already! Stop it with your head-games and smart-talk; it don't cut any ice with me. Next thing you're going to start the English lessons again."

15

McBain didn't appear surprised to see the bandage around my head when the hearings resumed, but he did acknowledge the shooting.

"I was sorry to hear of the unfortunate incident, Mr. Swager. I sincerely hope that the injury is not too serious. We can adjourn if you feel the need."

"Thank you, Senator, that won't be necessary. Canadians are notorious for being thick-skulled."

Balinsky's resignation had left an obvious vacancy on the committee, however McBain lost no time in introducing Isaak Weinstein as the new committee member.

"Security advises me that you have summoned reinforcements, Mr. Swager. Do you really feel that insecure?"

"Begging your pardon sir, I have no idea what you are talking about."

"Six armed private investigators is a bit of overkill even for someone as flamboyant as yourself, Mr. Swager."

Amelia turned and looked around the room. Covering

her mouth in surprise half whispering; "God Almighty ... a capo, a lieutenant and four guns. What the hell is he doing? Daddy is turning in his grave."

"Did you know about this?"

"Oh, Mickey, no, I swear to God, I didn't."

"Mr. Swager!"

"I beg your pardon Senator. I'll be with you in a moment. I had no knowledge of this."

"Why, Amelia?" He asked softly.

"I have heard whisperings about getting you into the family as a counselor. That capo was the last one, and since Daddy died, he has his own branch. The capo picks his replacement counselor for Mario."

"Mr. Swager. If you wish to take a recess, the committee will adjourn until you are ready."

"That won't be necessary, sir. I'm ready!"

"It seems, Mr. Swager, that wherever you go, someone is willing to harm you. Perhaps if you told us about the incident in Buffalo, it might shed some light on the matter, and your private army can leave."

"I apologize, Senator. The lady sitting next to me is the only private investigator I have hired. It's your turf and your problem."

"Hm ... strange, all are employed by a security firm owned by the Galante family. Is the shroud surrounding your mysterious life slowly unraveling?"

"Testifying here I must speak the truth, or the immunity clause is off the table. Only my safe conduct would remain in force. However, indicting me for perjury or some other criminal offense would leave the door open for my extradition. I'm not stupid enough to jeopardize my present status. I respect your intellect and your status as a member of this government, as well as your years, Senator. As my host, have the courtesy to respect mine."

The room waited silently for McBain's response. The small army of *Mafia* soldiers was like a double-edged knife. Leaving them, he could make me appear to be the gangster he had insinuated me to be, having them removed would give my statement credibility. He should have kept his mouth shut. I felt a little smug as I watched him deal with his dilemma. The committee members covered their microphones and whispered among themselves, then seemed to have come to an agreement. McBain summoned an aide to whom he gave some instructions, and in a voice louder than necessary, he called out to the security staff.

"Remove Mr. Swager's armed escort without further delay."

The spectators gawked as six men were escorted out of the room. The last guard walked to Mick's table and grabbed Amelia's arm. Not expecting it and not having time to object I jumped up and without warning drew my Colt pointing it directly at McBain, who instantaneously raised his hand to stop the guards. A mouse couldn't have moved without being heard. The guard let go of Amelia's arm as McBain's face turned ashen.

"Let your man touch her again and it is the last action you will take, Senator. Your blatant violation of the agreement gives me just cause. I'm tired of dodging your assassins.

If I use my weapon, I know your guards will take me down, but I'm determined to take you with me. Call them off! Your actions now force me to demand that my escort, as you call them, remain. First, you secretly declared war on me, and now you have done it openly. Patience is not one of my virtues, Senator, so I urge you. Decide!"

He brought the microphone closer to his mouth, raised his hand and rescinded the order. I holstered my weapon and sat as soon as the men returned. With the danger gone, the room erupted in chaos.

Only five men were escorted back in. Mick wondered about the sixth man. Amelia had counted six.

"You counted six guys they only removed five. What's up?"

"The sixth is the *capo*; he doesn't carry. Look to your right, tall guy in a tan three-piece suit."

She didn't bother looking when I did, but she searched for my hand, squeezed it and put it in her lap. I felt her stare until I couldn't ignore it any longer. Her soft brown eyes again declared her love and feelings without uttering a word. Her tough image was like her beauty, skin deep. I felt privileged being with her and proud that she was mine.

With the chaos subsiding, I contemplated the Senator's next move. He couldn't let my defiance of his authority or my charges of a murderous plot go unanswered. The resignation was an option, but that would insinuate his guilt.

"Can you give me just one good reason why I should not hold you in contempt, Mr. Swager?"

"Yes, although most likely one that is unacceptable to you. It is an American saying. You drew first blood."

"Cute response and it sounds familiar, but it doesn't apply here since no blood was drawn."

"I stand corrected. No blood was drawn. However, your order to have the lady removed by force, like a common criminal, was just as provocative. Considering your action, you can't possibly expect to be treated with the respect you demand."

"Disregarding the fact that the incident was an error by the security staff, we will call it a draw and continue, Mr. Swager."

"No, sir. Disregarding that fact, the buck stops with you. It didn't just not happen, the proper course of action is your apology to the lady."

"So be it. In the interest of justice and a speedy conclusion of the hearings, I apologize to you, Miss Galante."

Without looking at her, he grabbed his notepad appearing to read the next item on his agenda and proceeded.

"Have you ever been to Brazil, Mr. Swager?"

Bingo! He was getting down to business. Perhaps I was finally going to find out what he wanted, besides my life.

"Yes, sir. Many times, I do business in Brazil."

"When were you there last?"

"December 1973."

"Did you meet a man by the name of Geoffrey Savoy while you were there?"

"Yes sir, I did."

"Where? In Brazil?"

"The jungle, it is where I buy the logs to be shipped to Canada."

"Brazil is a big place, Mr. Swager. Half of it is a jungle. Could you be more specific?"

"No, sir. It wouldn't make any difference."

"It makes a big difference to this committee,"

"Not to me, Senator."

"Very well, what was the occasion for the meeting?"

"I'm sorry sir; I don't quite know what you mean by the question. As I stated, I went there on lumber business and had no plans to meet him; I didn't know him. The encounter was purely accidental."

"Well you see, Mr. Swager, the reason we ask is that he has been missing since that time and perhaps you have some knowledge of his whereabouts."

"Yes, sir."

"Well go on, Mr. Swager."

"Senator, I asked you at the beginning of the proceedings to ask questions. I am protected by the immunity, only when I answer questions. If I am to give voluntary statements, I will have to ask for an adjournment to seek clarification from my attorney, and you can understand how long that can take knowing the legal profession."

The room broke out in laughter, the Senator only affording a twitch.

"In that case, Mr. Swager, will you tell us everything from the time you met him until you last saw him?"

"Now that's a question I can answer, Senator."

The sarcasm of the statement wasn't lost

"Approximately two years ago while on business in the jungle in Brazil, I heard a child crying. It was odd because it was far away from a populated area. When I went to investigate and came closer to the crying, it abruptly stopped.

I stepped out from behind some bushes into a clearing and was confronted by an ugly scene. A man with his pants down around his ankles stood in the clearing. A few steps away a child was face down on the ground. Directly in front of my feet lay the man's jacket with a holstered gun placed on top of it. It didn't require a great deal of intelligence to deduce what had just happened. The man was startled at my appearance. I saw him look towards his gun, and we both made a move for it at the same time. He was at a disadvantage with his trousers around his feet and fell forward to the ground. I took possession of his gun and searched his jacket, while he remained in his disadvantaged state. He refused to identify himself and acted as if he didn't understand English. I picked the jacket up from the ground, and a pair of handcuffs fell out from one of the pockets. I used the cuffs to secure him to a nearby tree. I checked on the child, but her skull had been crushed. The rock that he had used was discarded next to her. It was covered with blood and hair. I checked for a pulse. She was dead. I estimated her to be around ten years old. This little girl had been raped and murdered by this man. When I looked at him, he grinned and said: "if I had known you were coming I would have left you some."

I couldn't control my anger and gave him a good kick. I would have preferred to shoot him but decided to give myself time to cool down. Awaiting his recovery from my kick, I searched the rest of his clothing. Among his belongings, I found his identification. It stated he was employed by the

DEA. To my surprise, I also found a photograph of myself. Needless to say, I was flabbergasted. He refused to give me any explanation. Because he had just raped and murdered a child, I felt perfectly justified in using any means to get the information from him. He eventually told me what I wanted to know. He had been sent to murder me and to dispose of my body, in any country other than the USA. With the evidence I had and no means of bringing him to justice, I found myself in a most difficult situation. Competent police investigators were days away. His training made me no match to ward off any attack, should I set him free. The fact that I was a witness to his crimes made him deadly. I felt I had been left no alternative but to kill him. I took his gun, forced the muzzle into his mouth and fired which necessitated me to leave the country immediately and return home without completing my transactions. These sir, are the facts as they occurred."

Throughout my statement, there had been dead silence. Everyone seemed to be holding their breath, afraid to make a sound.

A weight had been lifted from my shoulders. I had held back about the identity of the man who had hired Savoy. I thought of Belinda and hoped that her father would change his mind about me. It was his last opportunity for giving up, but McBain didn't crumble. Since I had refrained from divulging who had put out the contract on me, McBain obviously believed that I didn't know.

He continued. "Well now just a minute there, Mr. Swager, why would Savoy have given you any information?"

"Torture, Senator."

"You actually tortured the man?"

"Yeah … well, it wasn't really torture, more like threatening."

"Under the light of this new evidence we have to adjourn for today and continue tomorrow at nine."

I would now definitely have trouble getting through the hordes of people. As a result of my confession, the Senator must have realized this added danger and that it was in his best interest to get me past the reporters without giving me any possible opportunity to speak to them, or visa versa. He had a guard contact me to go through the hallowed, private hallway. It was no real surprise for my party and me to find him standing in the doorway of his chambers. He dismissed the guard.

"Could I have a moment in private, Mr. Swager?"

"I am sorry, Senator, you know that would be inappropriate."

He sounded defeated and conciliatory when he said: "Of course, you're right, Mr. Swager, I should have known better."

McBain watched me leave the hall.

Once back in the hotel I took a couple of the painkillers to stop the throbbing in my head, and I fell asleep. I awoke when Amelia kissed my cheek and started rubbing my back.

"I know that it has been rough, Mickey, but it will be over soon; won't it?"

"Knowing how lousy I feel, I'm sure you would have left me sleeping … there's something else isn't there?"

"Yes, Belinda McBain wants to see you. I told her that

you're not feeling well, but she is very insistent. I feel a little sorry for her. She looks awful."

"Okay, ask her to come in."

Belinda came in and looked back. She saw that Amelia was standing behind her. Amelia wasn't about to leave, and I didn't think that it was fair to ask her.

"I'll go down to the bar with Belinda."

"No Mickey, I'll go down to the bar. Call me when you're done."

Belinda sat in a chair by the window and cried. To control her sobbing, she took a deep breath and started to talk.

"I spoke to Mom about you. She knows you. She said that you know her as Maggie Lane."

I felt my throat closing, and it became hard to breathe. My heart skipped a couple of beats and then started to pound. I had difficulty regaining control. Belinda didn't appear to notice. She was on a mission.

"Mom is really upset. She told me that she treated you badly. I'm not sure what she means but I ... I don't know what to do. Please help me! Please talk to her?"

"Well ... I ... I ..."

"Are you okay?"

"Yeah, I'm fine Belinda."

"I would have come earlier, but I was at the hospital most of the day, I ... I ... I'm sorry ... I shouldn't have come. You have been through a lot; getting shot and all; I should have waited."

She got up to leave, but I asked her to stay. She hadn't just come to let off steam.

"Of course I'll talk to her."

"She picked me up from the hospital, and she's downstairs. I'll go down and ask her to come up."

In shock from Belinda's revelation, I was still anxious to see what had become of Maggie. I felt a little smug ... a bit arrogant. After all these years ... the beautiful girl who had dumped me needed me. So, Maggie was a part of this puzzle. My waiting was over. She was probably the link I'd been looking for. The knock on the door told me my waiting was over. She was there. I opened the door expecting to look back 17 years, but Maggie was not only lovely she was elegant. I invited her into the room and closed the door. Neither of us spoke. Her bottom lip quivered with uncertainty as she looked at me. I instinctively put my arms around her, and she immediately locked her's around my neck. I squeezed her tightly like a long-lost treasure, and I kissed her passionately.

The door suddenly swung open. Amelia stepped into the room. Standing with her feet as far apart as her tight skirt would allow. She held her gun in both hands with her arms stretched out menacingly. She didn't say anything but stared furiously with her gun pointed at Maggie's back. Her head was slightly tilted back, showing both her defiance and contempt. For a fleeting moment, I doubted the validity of her father's statement of, "no blood on her hands."

With her teeth clenched, she shook her head slowly from side to side and snarled, "you Bitch! I saw her downstairs, waiting for you, Mickey. I know how these things are done ... the brat she sets you up, and this one comes in for the kill.

They plan to whack you, and they are doing it for the old fart."

I didn't dare say a word. I was afraid to spook her. Her tension permeated the room and I knew that the least little thing would make her pull the trigger.

"I have loved this man since the first time I saw him, do you think that I would let you kill him now ... BITCH!"

Maggie stood frozen against me, not daring to turn around. Amelia continued,

"Like Mickey, I'm not afraid to die but I'm not ready to go yet. I have looked in his heart, and I shave seen the pain that you caused the man that I love. It is you who dies today BITCH! I'll get fried for it, but at least Mickey will be safe. I won't let you ruin his life anymore."

"Amie, please I beg you, take your finger off the trigger. Maggie's not here to kill me. She came to talk, as a friend."

"Kill ... talk, makes no difference. If I don't pull the trigger now, you'll go back to her. If I do, I'll be on death row. At least pulling the trigger gives me the satisfaction of knowing she's dead. She's still breathing because of you, Mickey. "

Feeling Maggie's hot breath against my skin, I also felt her fear. I took her arms from around my neck. She remained silent. I said gently, "Amelia, the bullets in your gun aren't hollow point and would probably go right through her, dropping me as well. Put the gun away, we both know that you can't keep it pointed at me."

Raising her arms, she pointed the gun at the ceiling and conceded, "you're too trusting, Mickey. Step away from her."

"I like it when you do that."

"WHAT!" she barked impatiently and flustered. "you like what?"

"I like the view. Raising your arms pulls your skirt up nice and high."

"Jesus Christ! Damn, it … you're unbelievable, certifiably nuts! How can you think of that crap at a time like this?"

"Yeah … well, it did the job of cooling you down didn't it?"

Maggie finally felt safe enough to talk.

"I don't want him hurt either, Miss Galante … I love him too. You were riding a tricycle when we were lovers. I was stupid to let him go, but that was a long time ago."

"Damn you. I won't listen to your crap! You had him, and you blew it, you married that farting pig. You hear that Mickey, she picked him over you and now she says that she loves you. Some friggin love!"

"I know I made a mistake. I wanted to rectify it, but when Belinda was born, I needed the security. When she was older, I tried to find Mickey. I wanted James to give me a divorce but stopped the proceedings when Belinda became ill. I had given up all hope of us ever getting together. James was spooked to the point that he became paranoid. If I had known there was any chance that he would actually harm you, Mickey, I would have warned you."

She covered her face and sobbed. I knew Amelia well enough to see that the crisis had passed, but her determination to keep Maggie away from me was as strong as ever.

"Amelia, I think I know what you must be thinking, seeing us together like this. But let me remind you of your promise to me. You said you understood and that you wouldn't stand in my way if and when I went to look for Maggie. Your promise still stands, and I'm holding you to it."

"That isn't fair, Mickey, that was a long time ago. Things aren't the same anymore. I thought that you loved *me* now."

"I do, but I also told you that I had to face my past and resolve it. This, right now, is part of the resolution. I want you to leave now. Please trust me, Amelia."

"I can't, Mickey, I can't just walk away and let her get her claws into you."

"You have no choice. This is my call."

She turned around and went to the door saying, "yeah … I gave you my word, and I'll keep it. It's a lot more than she did."

The door fell shut behind her. The fact that she was hurting bothered me, but unless I first came to terms with Maggie, I wouldn't be able to commit myself to her.

"There is more to the story you were telling me, isn't there, Maggie. Your husband has no intention of giving up. Before the smoke clears one or the other of us will be dead. Considering the resources he has, he may believe he has come out ahead, but it will cost him his political career and most likely his freedom for a long time."

"Oh, for God's sake, Mick, don't be so melodramatic. Nobody is going to die!"

"Why did you marry that toad if you loved me?"

She stopped and turned around, but didn't answer. Tempted, she held back.

"I have done things that I am not very proud of, and I would do anything to make it up to you, but I'm not here for me, I'm here for Belinda. She still needs her father, and you are destroying him."

"If that's true, you can start by telling me why there's a contract out on me. If you didn't know it before, you do now. By continuing to protect him, you're as guilty as he is. As it stands, it is entirely possible that I will leave this country in a bag."

"I told you, I mean you no harm but you refuse to listen to reason, and believe only what you want to believe. I'll tell you why if you'll listen."

"I'm all ears."

"James has his eye on the white-house and plans to run for the nomination."

"So what! I don't give a shit if Fatso wants to run the Boston marathon, I just don't want to die for it."

"He's gay."

"What?"

"James is gay. He knows that he doesn't stand a chance if anyone finds out. No one wants a gay President."

"Again, so what? I don't care what or who your President is."

"Okay here is the rest. I have already told you that I wanted to divorce James. When I had made that decision, I hired someone to find you, to learn all about you. That was how I found out you never married. I wanted to see if there was any chance of reconciliation. I never stopped loving you. James found out and was afraid that his secret would eventually be divulged. The idea of divorce didn't bother him. Quite the contrary, it was even acceptable. His manhood had been proven with the birth of Belinda. His real fear is if you and I were to get back, he believes I would eventually let the fact slip that he's gay".

"You knew all this? You knew, and never warned me? If you still loved me, why did you let it go on, you obviously knew where to find me?"

"I knew because the investigator I hired, found you in Montreal. He was to find you, not kill you!"

"Jesus Christ. Did I kill a man for that? This whole mess is all because your husband is a homosexual?"

I was furious, and she knew it, but she had come this far and couldn't leave without pursuing her goal.

"Is there anything left for us, Mick, or is it over?"

"Now that's a classic line, it sounds like something from a Peggy Lee song."

"Don't patronize me!"

"I'll damn well do as I please. I didn't come looking for you, remember?"

"Yes ... I know, but it is obvious I'm too late. You've found someone else."

"You know somehow I feel as if you are blaming me for this disaster. You ran off, and in spite of that, I have always loved you. You have been on my mind ever since the San, and it prevented me from enjoying any permanent relationship. You left so much unresolved. At the time, you said that you were leaving because you were scared. That I could understand, but when you didn't contact me, I began to feel that you no longer cared. I felt that you had taken the killing of Rodriguez as your opportunity to get out of your commitment to marry me … to get away from me altogether. I loved you so much … I would have done anything for you."

"I … I know how much I hurt you, Mickey, but I can't undo what I did. There was a lot more going on than you realize. Nothing has ever changed the way I feel about you. Why else do you think I tried to find you, and by the way, it's a lot more than you did. You could have found me just as easily if you had wanted to."

"Oh no, don't lay that one on me. I was a scared kid in love and with a dream."

"I know how beautiful Amelia is but you are someone who looks for more than that. We still have a chance. We're still young, and we can still be happy together."

"Yeah … I know, Maggie … I know, and that's what complicates things even more. Back in the San, you meant everything to me. You are a just as attractive today … but it has been 17 years …"

16

It was Tuesday morning and the events of the night before were still buzzing in my head. Maggie made her first appearance at the proceedings. I never expected to see her again, least of all at such a crucial time. It brought a whole new twist to the events. The mysteries were cleared up, and I finally knew what had motivated the Senator to have me killed. I had to rethink my strategy, how to deal with him. I considered McBain, my enemy, so I didn't mind bringing him down. But that wasn't all, whatever I did would also harm someone I cared for very deeply. Estranged as Maggie and I were, I still loved her.

Amelia had been very quiet during the night. She lay close to me and held me as if it were our last night together. She had done that same thing that last night in Buffalo.

I looked at her sitting beside me, and I couldn't help but feel proud to have her next to me. In contrast, I thought of Maggie and the Senator, and I snickered.

"What's so funny, Mickey? What are you snickering about?"

"Nothing."

"Don't tell me it's nothing, I saw the way you looked at her last night, and I didn't think it was at all funny."

"I wasn't thinking about last night. I was thinking about the Senator and Maggie together."

"Oh don't be so silly. I'm serious Mickey, especially after last night. I would think that you would be jealous of him."

"No ... strangely enough, I don't know why, but I'm not ... You still angry at me for last night?"

"No. I'm not angry at you, just scared I may lose you."

Staring at me, she probably expected my reassurance, but I couldn't give it to her because I didn't yet know what I was going to do.

McBain and his colleagues were late again, but that didn't matter because it was probably the last day of my testimony anyway. McBain's fence-sitting was over, he would have to move along and end it. He looked tired and old when he called the meeting to order.

"My colleagues and I have gone over your testimony, and we thought that we would give you the chance to expand on it, Mr. Swager."

"There is nothing to expand, Senator, but I am ready to answer questions if you have any."

He hesitated. I got the impression that he was ready to give up, to salvage whatever was left of his reputation. He must have realized that he was in quicksand. Shifting uneasily in his seat, he didn't look at me but stared down at his papers as if he were reading. I would have preferred him to continue asking questions, but the new committee member, Mr. Weinstein, took over.

"Did you happen to ask Mr. Savoy who had hired him, Mr. Swager?"

"I did sir, he was very uncooperative at first, but ultimately gave me the information."

"More torture, I suppose?"

"Was that a question, sir?"

"Forget it, Mr. Swager, just give us the name of the person who supposedly hired Savoy."

"Senator James McBain was the name he gave me."

The room fell silent. Weinstein looked at the Senator who stared straight ahead as if he hadn't heard my answer. Looking Maggie's way, I saw that she didn't even pretend to be shocked and could have warned her husband but apparently had chosen not to. Perhaps she reasoned a divorce would be easier to get if he were in prison. I knew that she didn't want me to tell the rest of the story. I couldn't see any point to it either; McBain was finished. He was anything but a stupid man, and he probably realized that to deny it would be futile. An investigation would prove once and for all that I was telling the truth. The danger to me was over.

Senator McBain stood up as if in a trance and slowly walked out of the room. Weinstein at a loss stalled looking down at his papers.

"I sincerely hope that you have proof, Mr. Swager, I personally find your accusation preposterous."

"Ask him, Mr. Weinstein."

The room erupted. Weinstein reached for McBain's gavel, pounding it mercilessly until some semblance of order was restored.

"Were there any witnesses when this took place?"

"No, sir. I was the only one present. I engaged the help of another person after Savoy was dead, but I can't disclose that person's identity."

"Cannot, or will not, Mr. Swager?

"Take your pick, Mr. Weinstein."

"You committed cold-blooded murder; you took it upon yourself to be judge, jury, and executioner, is that correct?"

"No sir, that is not correct. When members of the United States government send agents into another country with orders to kill, those are acts of war. I killed my aggressor to preserve my life. There was more than reasonable proof of my life being in danger. I had his confession it justified my actions."

"We only have your conversation on that. Maybe you are just making this up to get you out of this mess."

"There is no reason for me to lie. I can't be prosecuted for it, whether it was self-defense or not."

"Come now, Mr. Swager, this act of war reasoning doesn't apply here."

"You either conveniently didn't hear me, or you chose to ignore me. The US government has its own definition of war. It finds itself justified to enter another country, seize, maim, and kill under the pretense of the war against drugs, or a police action. The war that Senator McBain waged against me was very real. The United States government may not have sanctioned that action. How was I expected to know this? Had I not acted, I would be dead."

"We have no record of drug raids or any other activity in that country."

"Why am I not surprised? Of course, you have no evidence. Ask Senator McBain about it; he's the one who hired the assassin. You don't expect the Senator to publish his subversive acts, now do you? The fact that Mr. Savoy was there should tell you something, sir. I could if I chose probably assist you in finding the truth, but it is no longer any concern of mine."

"Mr. Swager, what reason could the Senator possibly have, to want you dead?"

"I can't answer that."

"Again, cannot or will not, Mr. Swager?"

"Again, take your pick, Mr. Weinstein. That's going to be the mess you guys have to deal with."

"We would like to know where his body is so his remains can be brought home and buried. We would appreciate it if you could tell us at least that much."

"He is already buried, although not at home. I don't know exactly where his grave is. That information could jeopardize the well-being of innocent people, and I do not consider the matter that important. Consider him missing in action."

Isaak Weinstein was silent and rubbed his chin. He was out of questions.

"Considering the events of today, we will adjourn. Mr. Swager, you will be informed about the next session of these proceedings within the next day or so."

"Don't bother Mr. Weinstein; I'm going home. My testimony is finished, and I have nothing further to add. Should you require further assistance in this matter, you can always come to me."

The guard knew the routine and led us through the back corridor. McBain's door was closed, but when they passed Weinstein's office, he was standing in the doorway. He was waiting for me and asked to speak to me in private. I asked Amelia to wait in the hall, and Weinstein closed the door.

"I am not entirely satisfied with your explanation or the outcome of your testimony. You were here to testify about your knowledge of the drug trade. I realize that drugs and violence go hand in hand, but there seems to be a different twist to this story."

"There is. The Senator wanted me here under the pretense of this drug inquiry. It was a convenient way to get me here since he knew about my acquaintance with the Galante family, in Buffalo. He wanted to find out how much I knew about him and the killer he hired. He could have come to me and discussed our differences in private."

"Were those differences great enough for him to have you killed?"

"Not in my mind."

"Okay, you've got my interest. What were those differences?"

"Off the record?""Yes, you have my word on it."

"I knew Mrs. McBain before she married him. We had an affair, and I suspect that I am their daughter's biological father. I guess that he feared I would let the cat out of the bag.

Politicians seem to think that the voters are equally as good at mudslinging as they are themselves. I don't believe that such disclosure will do anybody any good, especially the girl."

"So you'll be leaving Washington?"

"Yeah … I'll try to get a plane out of here first thing in the morning."

Mr. Weinstein and I shook hands and parted.

The parking lot was jammed with reporters. Cameras clicked as Robbie, with a stern-faced Mafia soldier beside him, inched the van through the waiting crowd. Amelia was sitting beside me holding my hand tightly. She didn't say anything, but I sensed her insecurity. It was as if she knew that with my business finished in Washington something was going to happen between us.

When we arrived at the hotel, I held her around her tiny waist, and we walked into the elevator. I felt her warmth, her uncertainty but most of all her love. I knew that I had some difficult decisions to make. The happiness of two people who meant the most to me would be affected. I could no longer imagine myself without Amelia. The temptation of Maggie was very real but was it enough to give up Amelia?

She helped me take off the holster. She unbuttoned my shirt, took off the vest and threw it on the bed. Bullets weren't on my mind anymore. The danger was over. I should have rejoiced at my victory but taking the Senator down as I said I would, wasn't as sweet as I had imagined. My victory was overshadowed by a sick feeling in my stomach. I had hurt Maggie and Belinda. I put my shirt back on while Amelia poured me a drink. She took my shoes off and told me to lie down for a while. I felt my head buzzing and dozed off.

I jumped up at a knock on the door.

"Damn," said Amelia, as she came out of the bathroom. She looked around the corner and saw me sitting upright.

"Go back to sleep Mickey; I'll get the door."

I heard Amelia unlock the door and heard Maggie's voice:

"May I please speak to Mickey, Miss Galante?"

"He's resting; I don't want him disturbed now."

"No, it's okay, let her come in, I'm awake."

Amelia opened the door wide.

"I want to talk to you in private if I may."

"Uh uh, Amelia is as much part of this now as you are. If you want to talk, you can do it in front of her; we have no secrets."

"Have you and I survived all these years, Mickey, to come to this moment? To come to the point where I can't even have my privacy with you?"

I let her continue.

"I love you, and I want you back. Everything is in the open now, and I can get a divorce."

"You lived a safe and comfortable life with James McBain and your daughter, while I slugged it out in the real world. I would say that you did a pretty good job of surviving, Maggie. Your husband is finished, and now you want me back?"

"You said last night that you loved me."

"Yeah I did, but I also said that I love Amelia; what about her?"

"She's much too young for you anyway. She'll get over this. You know that I can make you happy, Mickey, I did once, and I can do it again."

"Yeah ... she'll get over it as I did, but it only took me seventeen years."

"Mickey, we were both young then, but you were always more mature than I was in so many ways. We are a good match now."

Amelia remained quietly composed ...

"Look, I should feel flattered about this, but the fact is that one of you is going to be hurt and that makes me feel like shit."

Maggie continued.

"All the more reason for you to make a choice, isn't it?"

"Maggie, you can appreciate that I have been rather preoccupied these last few days. You'll have to give me time to work things out."

She was insistent:

"How much time?"

"After seventeen years another few days won't make a difference."

"Oh, Mickey ... you haven't the faintest idea how hard I tried to find you."

"I know how hard you worked, Maggie. You wrote a check for that investigator ... what was his name again?"

"Charles Douglas, but that ..."

"Right. I smashed his arm, that son-of-a-bitch. You went looking for me and hired Charlie. He reported back to you, and to your husband behind your back and that was what started the ball rolling. You led your husband to me."

"I didn't know!"

"I know that. But you have always known what McBain is, and you supported him right up to this very day."

"For God's sake! Not to kill you!"

"You found me, and you wanted me back, but you chose to stay with him instead."

"For Belinda's sake, not mine."

"Bullshit! You did it for the money, Maggie."

"Are you so different from the rest of us? Tell me, what would you do for money?"

"I work for it."

Amelia watched, quietly. Maggie came close to me and spoke softly with the voice that had once aroused me. She put her hand on my face and looked at me. I saw the chain around her neck. She saw me looking at it and pulled it out. She still had my ring. She still knew how to get to me.

"I have changed, all I ask is for you to take another look and give me a chance. I still love you, and I have your commitment, right here in my hand."

"I have taken a long, hard look, Maggie, believe me. I can't honestly say that I have no feelings left for you. I remember the time when we were both happy, but as far as my commitment goes, it became null and voided the day you left."

Amelia pointed to the vest and the gun on the dresser and said:

"Look, this is what Mickey had to put up with to stay alive."

"Dear God! Am I to blame for all this? Do you blame me for everything that is wrong in his life?"

"No," said Amelia, "not everything, he latched on to the daughter of the Mongoose. That he did all by himself... well maybe with a little help."

Maggie sat quietly at the foot of the bed and stared at the floor. Somehow, I felt sorry for her.

There was another knock on the door. Amelia went to open it.

"My God, this place is like Grand Central Station ... The brat's here," she said when she opened the door. "All we need now is the 'Old Fart, 'and we'll have the whole family. Maybe we should rent a suite so we can receive guests."

Belinda rushed to her mother; her eyes were red and swollen.

"He's dead ... Dad shot himself."

Maggie gasped:

"Oh God no! It can't be. He wouldn't do anything so stupid."

"He left a note. I don't know what's in it because the police took it."

She turned away from her mother and leaned with her back against the dresser biting her lip with her arms folded. She looked more angry than sad. Maggie was in shock and couldn't talk. Belinda spotted the gun on the dresser and grabbed it. Amelia saw her, but it was too late. She knew all too well how dangerous it could be trying to take it away from her.

To me, she wasn't a teenager. I saw only a gun in a hand that was capable of pulling the trigger.

"Easy Belinda, don't do anything that you'll regret. Shooting me isn't going to bring him back."

She started to cry and yelled.

"You killed him! You killed my father! It's your fault! I came to you for help and look what you've done!"

"He shot himself because he messed up. Don't you mess up too by shooting me."

She didn't answer, but I saw in her eyes that she was going to pull the trigger. I saw the flash from the barrel and heard the shot. It knocked me back into the chair. The pain was seconds away. I remembered the pain sequence from his previous encounter with a bullet. Who would have guessed that a young girl had just accomplished what her father's hired killers couldn't. I touched the place where the pain was most severe and felt the blood. I looked for Amelia. I wanted her to hold me.

Maggie screamed "Oh God! Belinda; you just shot your father!"

17

A gray-haired man holding a stethoscope stood beside the bed mumbling:"What a waste, what a waste."

"Turning to the nurse before leaving he said:

"Time of death was 9:22. Keep him on support. We're going to harvest a kidney for his daughter."

I saw myself lying in bed. Unconcerned, I followed the doctor to the waiting room where Maggie and Amelia sat, eyes swollen and sharing a box of tissues. Several men stood emotionless in and around the room. I recognized the tallest one as their *capo*. Maggie's last words to Belinda echoed in my head, "you just shot your father …".

Did Maggie want me back for a kidney or love? Not that it mattered anymore, but I was curious.

"Sorry folks," said the doctor in a hushed tone. "We tried. It looked like he was going to survive, but he took a turn for the worse. He just died moments ago. My condolences, I'm sorry for your loss."

I was right all along; death doesn't hurt; it was completely painless. The feeling of euphoria and freedom from the body was pleasant. If I could only see the white light …

The *capo* left, taking his men with him.

"I want to see him, Doctor," sobbed Amelia, "I'm his fiancée."

"Sure, I'll take you to him."

Amelia followed the doctor. She stood quietly beside My bed as tears rolled down her cheeks.

"You said that he was dead, but he's breathing, moving."

"No, that's the life support equipment. We're keeping him on it because we need a kidney for his daughter. His brain functions have ceased, and all his body functions will stop when we disconnect him. We'll remove his kidneys, one for his daughter and the other for a young man in Chicago."

"Like HELL you will!" she shouted. "Like hell! Disconnect him, and you'll be on a stretcher right beside him. Then you'll be sliced open for parts."

"Look, Miss … I know how you feel but …"

"But nothing! If he's dead, how come that he's moving his hand?"

"He isn't, what you see is involuntary muscle movement."

"Damn you! I've seen twitching stiffs; Mickey isn't moving like that."

The doctor bent over him, "Christ! He is!"

I began to feel something. Something was pulling me back towards my body. Being dead gives special powers, and I was supposed to be in control.

The doctor grabbed Amelia and held her back.

"Nurse, take her and get her out of here!"

As I came around, I felt the terrible pain in my chest. Opening my eyes slightly, I felt sharp lights stinging my eyes and became aware of a pounding headache. Perhaps it was better to keep them closed even though I sensed that people were standing near me.

"Is he coming around?"

"Naah … it takes a while. It looked like he was waking up when we brought him up here. Doc Simonds said that it could be days. They talked about this stuff in Med School, but I didn't think that Old Simonds would screw up like this."

"Christ, that broad was pissed-off at him. A hell of a looker. Wouldn't mind doing a physical on her and taking my time on the internal."

I lifted my arm. I saw a face through the slits of my eyelids. He took my hand and slapped it a few times and started calling my name. The experience from a previous awakening after surgery gave me an idea, and exaggerating my condition I whispered barely audible, "please … come."

Bending over me he answered, "yes sir?"

He wasn't the intern making the remarks about Amelia.

"No … Not you. I want the other guy."

"He doesn't want me, Steve, he wants to talk to you."

"Did you want me, sir?"

"Yeah."

"I'm listening."

"Yeah … so was I, moron!" I said swinging my arm with

all the power I could muster. My fist connected with his jaw because my hand hurt like hell. It didn't deck him, but I punched him hard enough to feel good about it. The pain in my chest was worth it, but my action triggered beeps and warnings from all the monitors. Once things were stabilized, the nurse officiously started to usher everyone out of the room. The tall *capo* Had returned, and he stood silently in a far corner with his arms crossed.

"Nurse, not him, I want him to stay. I need to talk to him."

"Mr. Swager, please, whatever it is can wait."

"Yeah ... well perhaps for you, not me. He is a priest, and I want him to hear my confession."

"He doesn't look like a priest."

"Yeah, I know it's his way of tending the flock ... undercover I mean, for The Lord."

The *capo* came over after she left. He leaned close.

"Good to see that you're doing okay, Mr. Swager. My name is ..."

"No name, no formalities, I know who you are. The intern I punched must be fired but not harmed. He is never to have a license to practice medicine because of his disrespect for my fiancée, and I want him to know who is doing this to him."

"There are easier ways to take care of him, Mr. Swager."

"Yeah, I know, but my way is better."

"As you wish."

I fell asleep but the soft hand of a woman lifting my head to let me drink awakened me.

"Hi Mickey, Do you know who I am?"

"Excuse me, Miss," said a man's voice. "Mr. Swager, do you know where you are?"

"Stupid question."

"Well … do you?"

"Course I know; in a hospital. The girl that I am going to marry is standing beside …"

I didn't remember what he said after that because I dozed off again until I heard the woman's voice again.

"Hi, welcome back Mickey, you sure scared the crap out of me. Bashing that intern caused some bleeding, and you had to go back to surgery."

"I don't know … everything is so hazy. How long have I been asleep?"

"You have slipped in and out of consciousness for the past three days."

"Good to see you, Amelia. I want to talk to you."

"Shh … you don't have to, I understand. I came to say goodbye."

"Why, Amie?"

"You have a daughter who needs you and a woman who loves you. I know when I'm licked."

"No wait, I … I don't want you to go."

"Damn, Mickey! What do you expect? This isn't the time to start playing games!"

"Oh God! Now that it's all over and things are decided, you call it quits. Are you getting cold feet?"

"Now just a friggin minute. First of all relax. Getting a heart attack or tearing more stitches won't do either of us any good. Look … maybe you have forgotten what you said.

I was standing in the doorway and Maggie was next to the bed when I heard you telling the doctor that you were going to marry her. Don't you remember?

"Ooooh … Christ! Was that Maggie? I thought that was you! Look … look, I'm fully awake, see? You have a mole right below your …"

"Okay, okay already, you're awake."

"Amelia, I love you. There is nothing more I want than to spend the rest of my life with you. Will you please marry me?"

She didn't answer, but she lay down beside me, hugging me gently and sobbing.

Amelia propped herself up on an elbow when the door opened, and a stern-faced nurse walked in and smiled. "Young Lady, I can appreciate your state of mind, but you have disconnected the leads to his heart monitor. The bed isn't big enough for the two of you, besides; there's another lady here to see the patient as well, so you might as well get off the bed."

Maggie walked in as the nurse was reattaching the leads to the monitor. Maggie looked disappointed when she said.

"I see that you have made up your mind, Mick. You are going to marry her."

"Yeah, you and I have only one thing in common now."

"What?"

"The daughter you kept hidden from me."

"I guess that I deserve that."

"You kept from me what was as much mine as yours. You have seen to it that she and I are strangers. I know it takes more than or a roll in the hay to be a dad, but you didn't even give me a chance."

"Is that why you are going to marry her, to get even?"

"No, that isn't it at all. I love Amelia. You only want me to be Belinda's father to get her off the kidney machine."

"That's not true! What a mean and vindictive thing to say!"

"It's the way I feel, Maggie but don't worry, Belinda isn't to blame, and she will get her kidney. I'm not pressing charges. The shooting was an accident as far as I'm concerned. Maybe in time, she will see things differently and forgive me for what she believes I did to her father. I don't want her to see me simply because she feels obligated. Donating a kidney is the least I can do for her after all she has been through. As far as you and I are concerned, you know me well enough to know that I would always have my doubts about you. I love Amelia, on the other hand, I know for certain now she loves me for who I am as I do her."

"Don't you play the martyr with me and don't you do me no favors, Mick."

"Double negative," snapped Amelia.

"What?"

"Don't and no in the same sentence ..."

"Yeah, yeah, yeah ... I see you're learning to play his games."

Maggie left just as Victoria Tang walked in. Maggie looked at her. She didn't seem surprised to see her. Amelia unable to control her joy ignored the new arrival. She wasn't quite finished gloating:

"Hey ... Maggie! You know something?"

"What!"

"The secret to keeping a man's interest is coming up with new ideas."

"Like?"

"Like this," she giggled raising her arms as high as she could."

Still giggling, she watched Maggie leave in a huff then she turned to face Dan and lowered her arms.

I felt myself go scarlet. Victoria came closer shaking her head and smiling.

"Who is this, Mickey?" asked Amelia, "another girl from your past?"

Victoria smiled: "Sweetheart, when you were still a baby he was peeking at the hemline of nurses' uniforms, or being more accurate, at their legs, as they were bending over beds."

"Now, this ... is getting very interesting. What else do you know, lady? I've been able to find out about most of him but his early years seem to be sort of ... non-existent."

"Yes ... don't I know it." Staring at me she continued, "he would have preferred being comatose some of those years."

"Are you the nurse who took care of him in that sanitarium?"

"Sanat*o*rium, my dear. A sanit*a*rium is a nuthouse. Come to think of it that place was probably both. But yes, I was his nurse for a while."

Victoria sat on the edge of the bed.

"It's a long story. He was very different when I first met him. He looked a bit like a dog with its tail between its legs.

Handsome and young, the nurses soon became aware of his interest in them.

The young ones enjoyed his ogling; the older ones could only envy them. I gave him hell a couple of times. He had developed the art of sticking his thumb under his arm to stop his pulse, and the nurse would keep holding his wrist. I became suspicious when Maggie put in a request for overtime on her nightshift two days after he arrived at …"

"Yeah … well look, Victoria, I'm surprised and happy to see you. It was nice of you to come by and look me up, but you don't have to go through my entire life. It's over … ancient history. Embarrassing me once in public was enough, wasn't it."

"Uh, uh, Mickey, embarrassment is a small price to pay if you are going to marry her. You see, Amelia, I knew how devastated he was when Maggie left him. Mickey is someone who doesn't take, or make, a promise lightly. He is always totally committed to those he makes, to the point of obsession."

Victoria no longer looked smug and amused; she stared harshly at Amelia. I have kept an eye on him for many years; because he is special to me. "The point being young lady, if you have committed yourself to him, his promise to you will be kept with a fanatical devotion."

"I haven't seen you for a long time, Victoria, but if you came to get me in trouble with her or with anyone else, I would have preferred you to wait a lot longer."

She started to fidget with her purse, and she looked uncomfortable.

"Nonsense, Mickey, you know I wouldn't do that. Hell no, I care and worry more about you than your own mother."

"Yeah ... well, that's easy, she's dead."

"I'm sorry to hear that. If not very loving, she appeared honest."

"Not even that, but thanks for the thought anyway."

"I'm glad that things have worked out for you. I came to close the last chapter of my life."

"Like hell, you're too damn stubborn to die."

"I see that Don Galante has left you more than his daughter; your vocabulary seems to have benefited as well. Anyway, I wasn't planning to stay this long. Perhaps I should come back some other time. Seeing you two happy, I can leave."

"What was that last chapter stuff all about? And how come you know so much about the Galante family?"

"For an intelligent man, you seem very dumb at times. Think about my being here. Do you think that it's by chance? I left the San when it shut down, and I moved back home to Washington, but I couldn't get you out of my thoughts. I was close to retirement and decided to look you up. The clinic in Montreal had your address, but you had disappeared, so I hired someone to find you. He did, and I have tracked you and your career ever since."

"Why?"

"Well, didn't I say at the train station, the day you left that I would stay in touch?"

"Yeah, but I didn't take you seriously."

"Well, you should have because I did. I must admit that you had me worried for a while."

"Worried? What, about getting shot?"

"No ..." she said as she sauntered over to the window. "No, I don't mean just the shooting. I mean your life. You might say that I've played a big part in it, but now, I like the result."

She stood back, leaning against the wall. Her eyes switched back and forth between Amelia and me.

"She *is* very beautiful isn't she?"

"Yeah ... she is, in many ways ... and you didn't have a damn thing to do with that."

With a smug but satisfied look on her face, she said, "Oh, didn't I. You'll have me to thank for some of the good as well as the bad. I sort of messed around in both your lives these last years, yours mostly, Mickey. I made some errors, but in this case, the end justifies the means."

"You're saying strange things again, Victoria, I've made my own choices."

"Ultimately, but like I said I had a hand in it. That Honduras thing almost turned into a fiasco. I didn't know that Raimundo was going to have you shot."

"You know about that?"

"Naturally, I arranged it."

"You arranged to do me in?"

"Hell no. No, that wasn't the plan. I only made sure that you handled the shipment."

"I don't understand this at all, Victoria ..."

"Come now, Mickey, you know that I don't lie. I have a younger sister in Honduras, Elizabeth Rojas. I asked her to do me a favor and arrange to have her husband ship those logs to Buffalo with you as the agent."

"Elizabeth is your sister?"

"Yes, she is indeed."

"HOLY shit!"

"You're right about that too, Mickey. She seems religious and often begs God's forgiveness for her sins. We stay in touch now and then ... I was a bit hesitant at first because I know how Virginia likes to flirt and I didn't want you to get too serious about her, but it was a risk I had to take."

Victoria smiled and winked. "She did, didn't she; you slept with her."

"Yeah ... well I ... I." Mickey felt himself go scarlet. "I ... not exactly ..."

Victoria suddenly jumped up. "She did it, didn't she; she promised that she wouldn't."

"No, no ... she didn't, honest. Virginia was nice, but nothing happened, honest."

"No, I didn't mean Virginia, I meant Elizabeth. She promised that she wouldn't. The SLUT! She promised me that she would leave you alone."

I was very uncomfortable because Amelia had heard everything. I had already admitted that there was someone else besides Maggie, but I hadn't planned to give her the details.

"You slept with Elizabeth, didn't you?"

"Yeah ... well, I ... I'm sorry, but I didn't know that she was your sister. She's ..."

"Oh God no. You don't have to apologize; it wasn't your fault."

She suddenly stared at Mickey in disbelief. "Oh God! You think that you seduced her, don't you?"

"Well … yeah, it wasn't difficult and her husband, well he …"

Victoria buried her face in her hands and burst out laughing. "She always was a bitch, even when we were kids. She probably stood in front of you and said: "*Will you love me? I know that it is wrong, but I want to be loved by a man whom I desire with all my heart*", while she stared deep into your eyes? Was that her line? Or did she say, "*how is it that love comes at such inopportune times*"? Or did she use both?"

I felt like a kid caught with a hand in the cookie jar. She knew her sister, and I knew that Victoria had seen right through me.

"Don't feel bad, Mickey. She's used that trick over and over again. She lets men believe that they are seducing her. She gets a kick out of it as well as a night between the sheets. I didn't think that you would fall for it, too. Her husband must have found out about it and sent a hit-man after you … for that, I am truly sorry. I knew that there was some risk, but it was the only way I could get you to meet Amelia. I didn't expect you to get hurt."

Amelia looked at Victoria puzzled and asked, "why did you want Mickey to meet me, I don't even know you, lady!"

"I know you don't. But I know you both. Mickey is special, and I wanted to keep him in the family. It took some doing, but all's well that ends well."

"In that case, you should have hitched him up to your slut sister."

Victoria shook her head. "No … I wanted him closer. I have known you since you were born, Amelia, and I also know your half-brother, Mario. He made sure that my plan for you two to meet would work. He didn't want to co-operate, but I knew about his involvement with dog-fighting. He had a few pit-bulls in the ring and didn't want your father to know. Your father always had more consideration for dogs than people. I contacted Mario and blackmailed him into making sure that the two of you would meet, according to plan."

"Then you knew my mother?"

Victoria smiled.

"Yeah … she held you in her arms, and she loved you deeply. You were her whole world. Amelia, your father, banished your mother and he did it easier than if she were one of his dogs."

"My father told me that my mother died giving birth to me. I thought that she was dead."

"She isn't, she is very much alive. Your father was a liar and a cheat. He had an affair with a young girl. His wife was less desirable to him with you at her breast. Your mother found out about the affair and wanted to leave with the baby. He let her leave, but he made her leave alone by threatening her parents who were still alive at the time. He said he would have them all killed if she didn't obey him. He kept you and made sure that you believed your mother was dead. Ever since your mother has felt like a coward for deserting her baby."

"Do you know where she is?"

Victoria wiped her eyes. Mickey had never seen her so emotional. Could it be that the flirty Elizabeth was Amelia's mother? There was a definite resemblance. Was that why I had always thought Amelia looked familiar right from the day she had kidnapped me? Elizabeth must have been very young when she had Amelia.

Victoria turned around burying her face in her hands trying to hide her tears. Amelia stood firmly beside me, holding my hand and watched her. She finally blurted out, "look here, lady, if you know where my mother is, you should tell me."

Victoria hesitated at first and then said, "HELL! … I have waited an eternity for this. I was always afraid that I would die before this moment. Now that it's here, I feel scared and cowardly, but you have the right to know."

"Is Elizabeth my mother?"

"No," she sobbed, covering her eyes once again. "Oh, God, help me! Elizabeth was the girl with which your father had an affair. Virginia is your sister, and I am your mother."

Amelia stood still for a moment and then slowly approached her. She took her hands away from her face and looked into her eyes. Then, she stroked her hair and said tenderly: "Mom, you're my mom."

Victoria smiled through her tears, and they put their arms around one another.

It was hard to see who was crying or who was laughing. After a while Amelia let her mother go and took her by the hand and led her over to my bedside saying:

"Mom, this is the man who is going to be my husband."

Printed in the United States
By Bookmasters